CAROL
HIGGINS CLARK

CURSED

A Regan Reilly Mystery

SCRIBNER

New York   London   Toronto   Sydney

SCRIBNER
A Division of Simon & Schuster, Inc.
1230 Avenue of the Americas
New York, NY 10020

First Scribner hardcover edition April 2009

SCRIBNER and design are registered trademarks of The Gale Group, Inc.,
used under license by Simon & Schuster, Inc., the publisher of this work.

For information about special discounts for bulk purchases,
please contact Simon & Schuster Special Sales at
1-866-506-1949 or business@simonandschuster.com

The Simon & Schuster Speakers Bureau can bring authors
to your live event. For more information or to book an event
contact the Simon & Schuster Speakers Bureau at
1-866-248-3049 or visit our website at www.simonspeakers.com.

Designed by Carla Jones

Manufactured in the United States of America

1   3   5   7   9   10   8   6   4   2

Library of Congress Cataloging-in-Publication Data is available.

ISBN-13: 978-1-4165-6217-7
ISBN-10:   1-4165-6217-6

Acknowledgments

Thanks to the help, support, and encouragement of the following, I could never feel cursed!

Roz Lippel, my editor.

Associate Director of Copyediting Gypsy da Silva, Copyeditor Patricia Nicolescu, Proofreaders Joel Van Liew and Steve Friedeman.

Scribner Publishing Manager Kara Watson.

Senior Production Manager Lisa Erwin.

Scribner Art Director Rex Bonomelli.

My publicist, Lisl Cade.

My agent, Esther Newberg.

My mother, Mary Higgins Clark, and my aunt, Irene Clark.

Thank you, one and all!

For Roz Lippel
My editor and friend
In celebration of the 13th book
we've worked on together!
With love

CURSED

Monday, January 12th

1

Snow and sleet were swirling in all directions as Regan Reilly steered her car onto the lower level of the Fifty-ninth Street Bridge in Manhattan, headed for Long Island City. This might not have been the best day to get ambitious about moving old files to a storage unit, she thought. The early morning had been cold and gray, with threatening skies and a prediction of what forecasters liked to call a "wintry mix" for later in the day. It wasn't even noon yet and the storm had arrived. It would have been a good time to hunker down indoors with a cup of tea or a mug of hot chocolate. But Regan was proud of herself for getting this far.

Ever since Regan had moved east from Los Angeles to marry Jack "no relation" Reilly, head of the NYPD Major Case Squad, her mother, Nora, had been asking politely, yet with increasing frequency, what Regan was going to do with all the things she'd stored in her parents' garage. "Now that the bad weather is hitting us," Nora had said the other day, "we'd like to be able to park both our cars inside."

"Okay, Mom, I'll take care of it," Regan had said, somewhat daunted by the thought of figuring out what to do with the remains of her life in Los Angeles. A private investigator, Regan still missed the small office that she rented in an old building in Hollywood. When she first walked in there, it had reminded her of the office building where her grandmother had worked on West Fifty-seventh Street in New York City. Black and white tiles on the floor dating from the year one, dark wood molding in the hallways, doors with thick, foggy glass, the feeling of a place from another era. Even its smell was familiar and comforting. Regan had been intrigued. She had the sense that the old walls held the stories and secrets of the people who had worked there over the years. Being of Irish descent, Regan had a special interest in tales of any sort. It was part of her genetic makeup. With thoughts of her grandmother, she'd signed the lease and never looked back.

But when it was time to leave, for what was a wonderful change in her life, she couldn't bear to part with her scarred old desk, her one-of-a-kind funky floor lamp, which she'd found at a yard sale at an old estate in Beverly Hills, and her battered file cabinets that the former tenant of the office left behind. To her they had a certain charm and would always bring back memories of her salad days as a PI. Among other things she kept was the thermos that she'd brought to work every day, filled with coffee. None of it belonged in Regan and Jack's newly renovated loft in Tribeca, where she had a home office replete with a custom-made cherrywood desk and matching wall-to-ceiling bookshelves, but to forsake these earthly possessions seemed impossible. They were like old friends.

"Perhaps we can turn the guest room upstairs into a replica of your western office," her father, Luke, owner of three funeral homes, had joked. "If you ever become president, we can turn it into a museum and charge admission."

"Dad, believe it or not, I have a sentimental streak."

"So did the Collyer brothers," Luke remarked, referring to

the brothers who lived in a brownstone on Fifth Avenue in New York City and became infamous after they died in 1947 thanks to their stunning inability to throw anything away. When the police received an anonymous tip that there was the smell of a dead body emanating from the residence, they tried to enter the house through the front door but were blocked by a wall of old newspapers, boxes, and piles of junk that you'd find on a street corner waiting to be taken to the local dump. A patrolman entered through a second-story window and found the body of Homer Collyer. It was presumed that his brother, Langley, had skipped town. Only after the authorities had spent a couple of weeks working to clear out the more than one hundred tons of rubbish from the residence was Langley's body discovered, just ten feet away from where his brother had been found, hidden under a pile of newspapers. After that any mention of the Collyer brothers brought to mind one heck of a mess. They even had a syndrome named after them.

Regan ignored her father's quip. "Living in the city, Jack and I don't have a basement or attic so I have no place to put this stuff."

"Thank God," Jack had joked.

Now all three of them were away. Her parents were in Palm Beach, Florida, and Jack had left yesterday for a law enforcement seminar in Miami. I'll show them, Regan had thought early this morning. She hadn't slept well. It was the first night Jack was away since they had been married. Funny how things change, Regan had thought. I was single until I was thirty-one and used to being on my own. Now that I'm with Jack, I feel out of sorts when he's not around. How easily one gets accustomed to a good thing.

After Regan crossed the bridge, she turned left on Northern Boulevard, and stopped at the light. She'd been down this road three hours ago after looking in the yellow pages and calling several storage companies. At Store Your Stuff they had a special deal on an available unit that was the right size and climate controlled. Regan had checked it out, filled out the necessary paperwork, then been fingerprinted.

"We don't want to do business with anyone who won't give us thumbs up," the receptionist had joked. "There's always a creep or two who'll want to use our facilities to hide ill-gotten gains."

"I can imagine," Regan had replied, thinking she should leave them her card. She'd then driven to New Jersey, loaded up her car with boxes and files, and headed back to New York. Maybe tomorrow she'd rent a van and get someone to help her load the unwieldy items like the desk and the lamp. Her mother was going to be so shocked when she returned from Florida.

When the light changed, Regan started to drive, passing a stretch of industrial buildings. A subway train went speeding by on the tracks above the road. After a few blocks the big sign atop Store Your Stuff's warehouse beckoned her. Here we go, Regan thought as she turned down a dead-end side street just past the sign, backed her car into the loading area, wheeled a cart up to her trunk, and started to unload. When she was finished, she pulled her car back out onto the dead end in case someone else with a Collyer brothers streak needed the space to drop off whatever junk it was they couldn't part with. Twenty minutes later, having deposited her precious cargo on the floor of her newly acquired rental property, and padlocking the door with a brand-new lock, Regan was stepping back out into the cold.

There goes a hundred bucks a month, she thought as pelts of what was certainly a wintry mix stung her face. She pulled her keys out of her pocket and hurried to the car. Her cell phone began to ring as she was opening the driver's door. She reached in her pocket again, grabbed the phone, and glanced at the caller ID. From the area code she could tell it was a Los Angeles number.

"Hello," Regan said as she gratefully sank behind the wheel and turned on the ignition.

"Regan, it's Abigail!"

"Abigail, how are you?" It was a question Regan was almost afraid to ask. A former neighbor, Abigail Feeney had moved into the apartment across the hall from Regan in a building in the Hollywood Hills not long before Regan moved back to New York. A hairdresser who worked in film and television, Abigail believed she'd been cursed since birth. Not only was she born on Friday the thirteenth, her parents had unwittingly given her a name that, combined with Feeney, added up to thirteen letters. In Abigail's book that was a bad start. Since then she'd had her share of unlucky things happen to her, including breaking her leg in the eighth grade just before a class trip, graduation, and all the swim parties. In high school she came down with the chicken pox right before her prom. As an adult she'd been unlucky in love more times than she liked to count. Shortly before Regan moved to New York, Abigail had met a guy she really liked. A guy that Regan instinctively didn't trust.

In October, Abigail had called Regan and told her that her boyfriend, Cody, had disappeared right after she lent him one hundred thousand dollars.

"He signed an IOU, Regan, that said he'd pay me back in three months. Then, a week later, I came home from work to find a note he'd left for me. He said he had to go out of town for a few days but he'd give me a call. That was five days ago and I haven't heard a peep out of him! And he won't respond to the messages I've left on his cell phone!"

"If it's a three-month IOU, then I don't think there's anything you can do just yet," Regan had told her.

In November, Abigail called Regan to tell her that she'd been injured on a movie set. A piece of scaffolding fell, knocked her over, and she broke her arm in two places. "Can you believe this Regan? I had to have surgery. They put pins in my arm. I obviously can't work, and the production company is acting like the accident was somehow my fault. I'm going to have to hire a lawyer. Furthermore, I tried to get in touch with you-know-who and his cell phone is disconnected."

Now it was a new year. Regan had called Abigail over the holidays but her home phone had also been disconnected. Regan didn't have her cell number. She braced herself for Abigail's answer to the state of her well-being.

"Regan! The no-good bum has been spotted in downtown Los Angeles. I desperately, and I mean desperately, need the money he owes me. The IOU runs out tomorrow, January thirteenth, which just happens to be my birthday. Can you please come out here and help me track him down?"

There was no need for Regan to confirm with Abigail the identity of the no-good bum. She remembered being in her apartment and seeing Cody Castle, the so-called producer, sitting by the pool, bent over his cell phone, text messaging nonstop. A good-looking guy who knew it, he was a little too impressed with himself for Regan's taste. She hadn't liked him and was quite sure that the feeling was mutual.

"Track him down?" Regan asked half-heartedly as cold air blew from her dashboard.

"Yes! I have to at least try. I didn't tell you where I got that one hundred thousand dollars I lent him."

Regan frowned, visions of loan sharks dancing in her head. "Where did you get it, Abigail?"

"My grandmother!"

"Your grandmother?"

"Yes. From the time I turned eighteen, she's been putting ten thousand dollars a year in an account for me. She wanted me to eventually use it for a down payment on a house or an apartment. I had every intention of doing that. But the other day she called and said she feels terrible that I had this accident and that Cody and I broke up. She's decided she's going to come out here and stay at her friend Margaret's condo on Kings Road in West Hollywood. Her friend is selling the place, and if it meets with my grandmother's approval, she's going to buy it for me. With cash! That cash is supposed to include that one hundred thousand dollars! If she ever finds out that I lent the money she scrimped and saved, and I do mean scrimped and saved, she'll kill me!"

A loan shark suddenly doesn't sound so bad, Regan thought. "When is she coming out?"

"Tomorrow. For my birthday! She's flying out from Indiana. I tried to stall her but she's already bought her ticket. I have to find him, Regan. I have to get my money back!"

Regan's feet were frozen, her nose was red, and Jack was out of town. Abigail had been awfully nice to her last winter when she had the flu, bringing her homemade chicken soup. Regan thought of her own grandmother and how hard she'd worked. I would never have wanted to face her if I'd lent one hundred thousand dollars of her money to some fly-by-night guy. "Okay, Abigail. I'll go home and check with the airlines. The weather's bad, but hopefully I can get a flight out tonight."

"Thank you, Regan! You won't be sorry. It's eighty degrees out here."

"I look forward to that. Oh, Abigail, I had tried to call you in December but your home phone was disconnected."

"Another disaster! The owner of my apartment returned from her adventure overseas. She gave the required thirty days'

9

notice. With a broken arm I had to pack up my stuff and get out of there before Christmas. Most of my stuff is in storage."

Regan blinked. Abigail and I will have a lot to talk about, she thought. "Where are you now?" she asked. "Where will we be staying?"

"I'm looking after three different homes whose owners are away. My primary duties are watering plants and collecting the mail. Don't worry. You'll have a place to sleep."

Terrific, Regan thought. I should have appreciated my lonely bed last night. "Okay then, Abigail."

"Okay, Regan. Call me when you book your flight. You have no idea what this means to me."

2

In the last three months, twenty-six-year-old Cody Castle had experienced such highs and lows, he thought nothing else could shake him to his core. He was wrong. Lying on a king-sized bed in a loft in downtown LA, staring up at the ceiling, his heart racing, he felt panicked. He couldn't believe Abigail's annoying friend Lois had spotted him. And of all the places to see her! Who'd have thought she'd be in a neighborhood bar in downtown Los Angeles late on a Sunday night? Last he remembered she lived out by the beach.

That Lois was a weirdo if he'd ever seen one. The night he met Abigail, she and Lois were together, parked on two bar stools at a club in West Hollywood. When he walked in, he'd been attracted to Abigail right away. She was pretty and had such a hip look about her. Her long, black spiky hair, her black skirt and boots, her black fingernails, her dark eyes that contrasted with her light skin. Cody knew he wanted to talk to her, but he also knew he'd have to put up with her friend, who was wearing long red gloves up to her biceps. Hey, it's West Hollywood, he thought as he struck up a conversation.

Lois jumped in, explaining in excruciating detail how an agent had spotted her beautiful hands and gotten her a job as a hand model in a commercial. She'd made good money and now that her "paws" were in demand, she'd decided that they would never see the light of day again. Sunshine on your shoulders might make you happy, but on your hands it causes freckling. She'd always always always wear gloves in public, would never shake anyone's hand ever again, and her days of doing dishes and emptying the garbage were long gone.

This girl is nuts, Cody had thought.

"I'm jealous," Abigail had said with a good-natured laugh. "I'm a hairdresser. There's no way I can treat these hands with kid gloves," she said, holding them up.

Flirtatiously, Cody had grabbed them. "I think your hands are beautiful," he'd said as Lois glared at him. "Can I buy you two a drink?"

Ten minutes later, his writing and producing partner joined them. Dean got stuck talking to Lois while Abigail and Cody had eyes only for each other.

The next night Cody and Abigail went out to dinner, and before long they considered themselves a couple. Neither Lois nor Dean had any interest in spending time with the happy twosome or with each other. Cody had never laid eyes on Lois again until ten hours ago. Propelled by fear, Cody jumped out of bed. What was she doing downtown last night? He glanced out the window at the sunny day, wishing he could go out for a jog. Shouldn't she have been home with her sink full of dirty dishes and over-flowing garbage can? Feeling cooped up, he'd gone down to the corner bar for a beer. It was late and he was staying downtown, a fair distance from his old stomping ground. He felt sure he wouldn't run into anyone he knew. As he was approaching the door to Jimbo's, he'd seen her sitting at a table next to the window. Before he even saw Lois's face, he knew it was her. The minute he spotted a woman's gloved hand lifting a drink, he'd stopped dead in his tracks. But it was too late. She turned and saw him. As her eyes widened he bolted, hightailing it back to the loft where he was supposed to keep a low profile. He knew Lois would call Abigail, and knowing Abigail she'd organize a search party. With Lois at the helm. He could tell her type. She'd seek revenge on him not because he owed Abigail money, but because he'd preferred Abigail in the first place.

Cody rubbed his eyes. He'd barely slept. What was he going to tell Dean? He'd already put him through the wringer. He and Dean had so many plans for their short film, a film that they were sure would put them on the map. Plans that were almost derailed three months ago when Cody called Dean from jail. Dean hadn't taken the news well.

"You were thrown in jail because of unpaid traffic tickets?" he'd screamed.

"I also had a little problem with my insurance and expired license."

"What's wrong with you?"

"I was trying to clear things up. Remember that movie I worked on last year in Texas? I hated every minute of it. I ended up getting a lot of traffic tickets. They piled up. I flew down here to get things straightened out and was going to fly right back but the judge wasn't happy with me because I missed a court date. So he threw me in the slammer."

"For how long?"

"Sixty days."

"Sixty days! What about our movie? We wanted to shoot it in January! It's set at a ski lodge in Vermont, for God's sake! My friend is lending us his house. He's not going to let us use it all winter. Cody, we wanted this movie to be ready to show at the film festivals in the spring."

"Don't worry. I'll be out before Christmas."

"What am I going to tell people? We're co-directing this!"

"Tell them I'm off tinkering with the script."

"What about Abigail?"

"I can't tell her. If she finds out I'm in jail, she'll want her money back now. I paid off my credit cards, and my court fines were high. Whew! Really high. She'll sabotage our film. Listen, the IOU isn't up until January. I'll worry about it then. Hey man, we're going to do so well with this film, I'll pay her back with big interest. A little late, but I'll pay her back."

"Yeah, sure. What if she calls me?"

"She doesn't have your number. She doesn't know where our apartment is, only that it's in Malibu. How many times did you see her, once after we met? She won't know how to find you. When you think about it, it turns out to be a good thing she was away on location so much after we started dating. When she was home, we wanted to be alone."

"Your long-distance romance brought tears to my eyes."

So while Cody was in jail lifting weights, Dean ran himself ragged handling all the logistics of the project. He set up an office in his mother's basement in Fort Lee, New Jersey. He cast New York actors. He was running low on money but found investors in Los Angeles who wanted to meet both directors before they handed over their checks. That's why Cody had to risk being back in Los Angeles for a few days. Dean had borrowed a friend's loft for Cody to stay in downtown. Cody was supposed to keep out of sight except when he had to surface for work related appearances. Kind of like Lois's hands.

The movie was scheduled to start shooting next week.

Clad in his boxer shorts, his physique rippling with muscles he'd built up in jail, Cody decided he'd better try to eat something. He strode to the kitchen, a large space with gleaming granite counters, state-of-the-art pots and pans hanging from a rack above the center island, and an eight-burner stove fit for a professional chef. What a joint, Cody thought as he poured himself a bowl of cereal and cut up a banana. A friend of Dean's had bought this place before it was renovated but was hardly ever there. He spent most of his time in New York.

Cody sat at the counter and started to eat. Out of jail for almost a month, it still felt good not to have to eat with a plastic spoon. But at the moment he still felt like a prisoner. That would end as soon as they got the rest of the seed money and headed out of town. And once the movie was in the can, everything with Abigail could be worked out.

The sound of a key in the door made him flinch.

"Hello," Dean called cheerlessly as he let himself in. Three seconds later he appeared in the kitchen. The sight of Cody's brawny chest and arms annoyed him to no end. As usual, Cody would continue to be the one to attract women. Dean felt like a nebbish. He knew that he was scrawny, nondescript, and nothing to swoon over. That's why he was so anxious to prove himself with this movie. The script he and Cody had written together was funny and scary and clever. If he could put up with Cody for the next several months it would all be worth it.

"Hey," Cody said. "You want some cereal?"

"No, I've already had a bran muffin. What's wrong?"

"What do you mean 'What's wrong?' "

"I can tell something's up."

Cody cleared his throat. "As a matter of fact . . ."

Dean threw down his bag, a bag filled with notes and files and scripts and every last scrap of information having to do with the movie. "I can't take it!"

"Take what? You don't even know what I have to tell you."

"Let me tell you something, Cody. I've been working my butt off to keep this project going. I just want to get it done. I'm at the point where I don't know what I'd do to someone if they tried to stop it!" The veins in his throat were bulging. His hair was falling in his face. His slitty eyes looked bloodshot.

"Chill out," Cody said. "It might not be so bad. Last night I went to have a beer at the place on the corner. Who did I see but Abigail's friend sitting right there. The one with the gloves."

Dean slapped his hand on the counter. Another bad memory! The night at the bar when he'd had to listen to her talk about how her hands were really two little actresses she'd named Meryl and Angelina, while Cody was whispering sweet nothings in Abigail's ear. He'd wanted to scream. Now Dean felt like he was at the end of his rope. "That woman is insane! What were you doing out? I told you not to go anywhere!"

"I was in jail for sixty days. I get cabin fever very easily."

"You've been out of jail for weeks. This was only going to be a few days of house arrest!"

Cody's new cell phone rang. It was over by the bed across the room. "If you'll excuse me," he muttered.

"Don't answer it if you don't recognize the number!" Dean barked.

Cody grabbed the phone off the bed and when he saw who was calling, he knew it wouldn't make Dean happy. It was Stella. Gorgeous Stella whom Dean had gotten to read the script. Stella Gardner, who was a hot young actress getting more famous by the minute. She was on a series that filmed in New York and had been interested in playing the lead but like the investors, wanted to meet the other director first. When Cody was sprung from jail, he'd flown to New York where Dean had set up a meeting for the three of them. She'd promptly fallen in love with Cody. He was barely out of his orange jumpsuit and she was inviting him to spend a quiet Christmas with her mother and father on their ranch in Texas. He would have gone anywhere with her, even to the state where he'd just been incarcerated. And he did.

"Hello there," he said, trying not to sound too mushy. At this point it was no good rubbing it in Dean's face. He mouthed "Stella" to Dean, who rolled his eyes.

"Well, hello yourself," Stella purred. "I just miss you too much."

"Me, too," Cody said. "Uh, Dean's here. We're just working away."

"Well, I've got great news. I just wrapped for today and I'm not working again until Friday. Then we'll be off to Vermont! But I can't wait that long to see you. I'm flying out tonight so we can be together."

Cody's stomach dropped. Stella's series was becoming more and more popular. With all those gossip show reporters lurking around every corner, there was no way he could stay out of sight if they were together. As it was, he'd been telling her in New York that they shouldn't go public with their relationship just yet. Not until the movie finished shooting. It would seem like she got the job because she was the director's girlfriend, blah blah blah. "I don't know whether that's such a good idea."

"Don't you miss me?"

"Of course. Of course I do. I just don't know if I'll be able to pay enough attention to you. We have so much to still get done. And Dean has been working so hard." Cody hurried back to the kitchen and jotted the words SHE WANTS TO FLY OUT on a piece of paper.

Dean read it, sunk onto a stool, and put his head down.

"He was working hard but so were you. You were all by your lonesome toiling away on that great script," Stella said sweetly. "I can't tell you how much I admire that. Cody, I really want to see you."

Cody swallowed hard. Stella was the reason Dean had been able to line up more investors. But she thought they had all the money in place. If she dropped out now, they'd have no movie. He had to do what she wanted. "Okay then. Did you book a flight?"

"Yes. It leaves New York at six and gets in a little after nine—Voyager Airways. I can't wait to fly into your arms! And I can't wait to see what that downtown loft is like. The way you described it on the phone last night made it sound fabulous! Downtown Los Angeles is getting more and more exciting."

"It sure is," Cody agreed. "I'll see you tonight."

3

Back at her loft, Regan hung her jacket in the closet and kicked off her damp shoes. It was so good to be home, at least for a few hours. Walking through the living room, she smiled at the sight of a favorite wedding picture. She and Jack were coming down the aisle of the church, her arm through his, both looking so happy. In the pews, their friends and families were clapping for them. At the time, Regan had been thinking that she should have been the one leading the applause.

Meeting Jack was truly a miracle, Regan thought as she headed into the kitchen. And the more I hear about guys like Cody Castle, the more Jack feels like the Miracle of the Century. I'm sorry it took Dad being kidnapped, she thought, but he loved to take credit for bringing Jack into her life. It had become one of his favorite stories. As head of the NYPD Major Case Squad, Jack had been in charge of the investigation. In the process of getting Luke back, he and Regan had fallen in love.

Regan filled the kettle with water and as she waited for it to boil, her thoughts once again focused on Cody Castle. What did he expect to get away with by taking that money from Abigail and then disappearing? If he were really making a movie, then how could he expect to avoid Abigail forever? Hollywood was a small town and she was in the business. What was he doing in downtown Los Angeles? Had he been there the whole time? After Abigail had called her in the fall, Regan had Googled Cody Castle but hadn't come up with anything significant about the Cody Castle she was interested in.

When the kettle started to shriek, Regan fixed her tea then walked down the hall to her office. She sat at her computer, logged on, and found a flight that left for Los Angeles at 6:00 P.M. on Voyager Airways. So far, it hadn't been delayed.

She called Abigail and gave her the details. "I'll be there, Regan. I can't thank you enough. For some reason I feel like my whole life is on the line."

The words gave Regan a funny feeling. "It's not your whole life, Abigail. If she has to, your grandmother will get over it."

"You haven't met Grandma."

"No, but I guess I will."

"She's packing her bags as we speak. Thank God she's staying with Margaret. They're so excited that they're going to be spending time together. We're going to have to make something up about why you're around."

"I know. Don't worry."

Regan hung up and called Jack, figuring she'd just leave a message. To her surprise, he answered.

"Regan!" he said. "We just broke for lunch. How's it going?"

"Okay. I have a few things to tell you, some may surprise you."

"Uh-oh. I'm all ears."

"First of all, I rented a storage unit in Long Island City and have already started moving files there."

Jack laughed. "That doesn't surprise me. I knew you had it in you."

"Second, I could barely sleep last night without you here."

"That doesn't surprise me either. I didn't sleep so well my-self."

"And third of all, I'm flying to Los Angeles tonight."

"What?"

"Gotcha." Regan laughed. She'd already told him about Abigail's calls in the fall. "I heard from Abigail again," she began, then explained to him what was happening now.

"So what are you going to do if you find this guy?"

"I have the feeling that Abigail will do whatever it takes to get him to hand over the money. If he still has it." Regan sighed. "She's pretty upset about the thought of her grandmother find-ing out she lent anyone that money."

"Regan, be careful. You don't know what this guy is capable of or who he might be hanging out with."

"I know. We'll be careful."

"You couldn't stay home alone without me?" Jack teased.

"That's right. This is all your fault."

"Don't let your mother get that idea."

"In her book, you can do no wrong."

Jack's voice turned serious. "How long will you be there?"

"I won't stay more than a week. One way or another it will have to be over by then. If Abigail doesn't get the money, I can't imagine she'll be able to stall her grandmother much more than that. She's arriving tomorrow."

"I hope you find him, get the money, and are home by the weekend."

"Me, too. Believe me."

When Regan hung up, she tried her mother's cell phone.

"Hi, honey," Nora said. "I hear you're getting some snow up there."

"A bit. But I'm flying to Los Angeles."

"What?"

Sitting by the pool at the Breakers Hotel, Nora listened intently. "Regan, isn't Abigail the one who thinks she's cursed? The one who everything happens to?"

Why did I ever tell her that? Regan wondered. "Yes, Mom. She's the one."

"Oh, dear."

"She needs my help. Can you imagine me ever having to tell Nana that I'd lent a hundred thousand dollars she'd given me to a guy, never mind one who then left me?"

"I can't believe you'd ever be that stupid, Regan."

"Thanks for your vote of confidence. Poor Abigail. She thought she'd finally found 'The One' and they had a future together. She's a good soul. I barely knew her when she insisted on bringing me chicken soup when I had the flu last year. She had just moved in."

"Bringing chicken soup across the hall is one thing. Flying three thousand miles to hunt down her crazy ex-boyfriend is another."

"I didn't pay her for the chicken soup. She's paying me."

"Well, that's something at least. It's too bad Jack is away. You might not have said yes if he were around."

"Mom, you're psychic. Jack knew he'd get the blame for this."

Nora laughed. "Regan!"

"Is Dad there?"

"He's golfing."

"Give him my love. I've got to pack. I'll call you from L.A."

"Be careful."

"Jack said the same thing. What a coincidence."

When Regan hung up, she called a car service and arranged for a pickup. She then pulled her suitcase out of the closet. Four hours later she was waiting in line to check her bags at the curb at Kennedy Airport. The beautiful young blonde standing in front of her looked familiar. Who is she? Regan wondered. Then it came to her. She was a new young actress who plays an investigator on one of the popular crime series. Regan had seen it once and had been impressed by her acting. Inwardly, Regan smiled. Maybe I should ask her what she'd do to hunt down Cody Castle.

4

Margaret Suspack was sitting at her dining room table, paying her bills, a cup of coffee, a crumb bun, and a calculator by her side. She wanted to get paperwork out of the way before her friend Ethel Feeney arrived tomorrow. Eighty-two years old, Margaret, known to her friends and family as Mugs, had a pleasant face, a roundish figure, hazel eyes, and a bouffant hairdo she kept in a soft shade of honey.

After her husband, Harry, died a few years earlier, she'd been outraged by the number of snake oil salesmen who thought they could take advantage of her because she was alone. They couldn't, and she'd developed an even steelier spine toward anyone who wanted her to part with her money. For any reason at all. And forget anyone who thought she was an easy target for a scam because she was elderly. She was prepared for them. The young man who called recently pretending to be her grandson and saying he was in trouble and needed her to wire money to people who were going to hurt him could never have expected her response. Mugs blew the whistle she kept by her bed in his ear. "You ought to be ashamed of yourself trying to fool old folks," Mugs had sputtered before hanging up.

Mugs had no children or grandchildren.

Harry would have been proud of her, the way she was taking care of herself after he died, but he wouldn't have been surprised—Mugs had always been thrifty and resourceful.

We had such fun at this table for so many years, Mugs thought as she studied the wattage count of her electric bill, comparing it to the previous month's. Harry had worked as a lighting director since the early days of television. Because they were never blessed with children, their friends became like family to them. The chairs around their table were often filled with neighbors joining them for anything from spaghetti topped with Mugs's delicious sauce to an impromptu potluck supper.

Mugs had worked four days a week as a manicurist. She loved the gossip that emanated from the salon. When she and Harry entertained, she told stories about crazy clients and Harry filled them in on the shenanigans of celebrities on the set.

But over time things slowed down. Harry retired, and the old-fashioned beauty parlor closed, victim to the decreasing number of women looking for a wash-and-set. Salons that offered blow-drys and music that would burst your eardrums were the rage. And as it goes, many of their friends had moved away after they retired. Some had died. Then Harry had taken his final breath a few years ago. "Lights out, Mugs," he'd said on his deathbed. God love him, Mugs thought. No matter how sick he felt, he always kept his sense of humor.

Mugs never thought she'd leave Los Angeles, but after spending Thanksgiving with her sister in Florida, surrounded by her nieces and nephews and their children, it had been hard for her to come back.

"Mugs, let me make a suggestion," her sister Charlotte, known as Charley, had said when she dropped her off at the airport. Their parents had been big on nicknames. "Sell the apartment and move down here with me. I don't like to think of you being so far away by yourself."

"I'm not by myself," Mugs had insisted. "I still have friends."

"I know. But I wouldn't mind moving into one of those adult communities and I'd rather do it with you. They're supposed to be a lot of fun."

"From what I've read, some of those adult communities are a little too much fun," Mugs said primly. "I don't want to meet a man. Harry was it for me."

"That's not what I'm talking about. There are a lot of group activities like bingo and Ping-Pong. Mugs, I miss you."

When Mugs returned to her apartment, she'd felt lonelier than she ever had. A few days later, she'd called her sister. "Charley, I hate to say it but you're right. It's time for me to join you in Florida. I have to sell my apartment first and I don't know how long that will take. It's tough these days. I'm not leaving here until I have the money in the bank."

"Mugs, I'm so happy!" Charley had said. "I'll start looking . . ."

"I'm not signing up for anything until I've sold this place . . ."

"I know. I know."

Mugs had contacted a real estate agency that sent out a young agent to size up her apartment. Mugs had been appalled by the little whippersnapper, with the way she insulted Mugs's home, implying it was a dump just because it didn't have granite counters or Jacuzzi bathtubs or newfangled appliances. It was neat and clean, no paint was peeling, and the ceiling wasn't about to cave in. For forty years, it had been good enough for Mugs and her Harry. All four rooms had sliding glass doors that opened onto a terrace. The terrace overlooked a lovely courtyard with palm trees, flowers, and a swimming pool. Mugs's guests often commented that it felt like a resort.

"If you want to get more money," the twenty-something had said, twirling her streaked hair and teetering on six-inch heels, "you should totally update your property before you put it on the market. It's, like, so worth it. I know a guy who makes amazing cabinets . . ."

"Listen, young lady," Mugs had said, her eyes blazing. "At this point of my life, I don't want to waste whatever precious time I have left picking out 'amazing' cabinets I will never use, and then sitting here waiting for workmen who never show up on time. Anything I update will be changed by whoever buys it anyway. Thank you for your time!"

Mugs then called another real estate agency. A young man arrived within minutes. "You'd think I'd called an ambulance," Mugs had remarked when he walked through the door. But at least he seemed to have people skills. He told her the market was tough, but they'd do what they could to find the perfect buyer. "Plenty of people would just adore this apartment the way it is," he'd assured her.

"You're darn tootin'," Mugs harrumphed.

"May I call you Margaret?"

"No, you may not."

Over the next month, a few stragglers came around and poked through her closets. One made an insulting offer that sent Mugs through the roof.

"This might not be Buckingham Palace, but it's not skid row either," she'd told the agent.

"You're absolutely right, Mrs. Suspack."

Christmas rolled around and she and Ethel Feeney, her childhood friend, had their annual chat. They'd had such fun together in high school, and had been co-treasurers of their class senior year. Even though they hadn't seen each other much over the years, they had stayed in touch. Mugs told Ethel about her hopes to move to Florida before long, and Ethel had filled Mugs in on her granddaughter Abigail's accident on a movie set.

"That's too bad," Mugs said. "Does she want to buy an apartment?"

"She does but she can't afford it yet."

Over the holidays, Ethel had become concerned about Abigail. She'd come home to Indiana for a week and seemed stressed the whole time she was with the family. It was understandable because she'd been through some tough times. She suffered a broken arm and a broken relationship. The relationship she didn't want to discuss at all. In the past, Abigail had always at least pretended to laugh it off when things didn't work out for her with someone she'd been interested in.

After Abigail went back to Los Angeles, Ethel was trying to think of something special to buy her for her birthday. Then she'd had a dream that something terrible happened to Abigail. When Ethel awoke, she couldn't remember exactly what it was but was very upset. Always superstitious, a trait she'd passed down to her granddaughter, the next morning she called Mugs. And as they had in high school when they were in charge of the funds in their class treasury, they'd haggled over how much something was worth. In this case, of course, it was Mugs's apartment.

"It's a little difficult because I haven't seen your place in twenty years," Ethel said. "Not since you had that retirement party for Harry."

"We had fun, didn't we?" Mugs said. "Who'd have thought so many people would end up in the pool? Listen, Ethel, spend the money on an airline ticket and come out here for a visit. Stay with me. That way you can inspect this place from top to bottom. Then you can decide if you want to spring for the perfect birthday gift for your granddaughter."

Ethel laughed. "Don't forget, Mugs. I'd pay you in cash. No waiting for loans to be approved. That should count for something."

"Cash talks," Mugs said agreeably. "As long as there's enough of it. No matter what, we'll have a good time."

"If we don't kill each other."

They both were excited. It had been so long since they'd spent time together. And if everything worked out, the two of them would be thrilled to avoid the broker's fee.

As Mugs put a stamp on the envelope of her electric bill, the phone rang.

"Hello," she answered as she glanced out the sliding glass doors. It was late in the day, and the lights around the swimming pool had just come on.

"Mugs, it's Walter."

Mugs rolled her eyes. Walter was the Casanova wannabe at the local senior center. He was always trying to get her to go out dancing with him. She had zero interest in such activity.

"Hello, Walter. What's up?"

"Mugs, they just found Nicky dead in his apartment."

Mugs sighed. These kinds of calls were getting too frequent. "That's a shame, Walter. He's been so sick lately, maybe it's a blessing. Did he die in his sleep?"

"He didn't die in his sleep, Mugs. He was murdered."

5

The pilot's voice came over the speakers. He began the usual spiel that frequent flyers could recite in their sleep. "Ladies and gentlemen, in preparation for landing, please . . ."

Regan breathed a sigh of relief. She'd read for several hours on the plane, then tried to doze, but it was only on overnight flights that she ever was really able to lose consciousness. Now it was nearly midnight East Coast time and she was tired. The last hour of the flight from New York to Los Angeles was always a drag, but tonight she felt more restless than usual. If Cody Castle was still in Los Angeles, Regan had the feeling that every minute counted. She leaned toward the window and looked down at the lights that seemed to spread out for miles. Normally an exciting view, tonight it was discouraging. Cody Castle could be anywhere.

Little did Regan know that up front in first class someone else was looking out the window, also consumed with thoughts of Cody Castle.

When the plane landed, Regan turned her cell phone back on and checked her messages. There was a message from Jack saying it was 10:30, they just had dinner at the hotel, and he was going to bed. "I love you. Call me if you need anything, otherwise I'll talk to you tomorrow."

Regan would have loved to talk to him now but she didn't want to wake him. Suddenly her life in New York felt very far away.

The other message was from Abigail. "I'm sitting in the car at a waiting area at the airport," she said. "As soon as you get your bag, give me a call. It'll only take me two minutes to get there and we can get right out. If I park the car in the lot, it's such a hassle."

Sounds good to me, Regan thought as she started to gather her possessions. The guy stuck in the middle seat turned to her and smiled. "Again, I'm really sorry for what happened."

Regan laughed. "Don't worry about it."

After settling in their seats before takeoff, he'd pulled out his breath spray, opened wide, and squirted. Half of it spritzed the right side of Regan's face. At least he's a guy with good hygiene, Regan had thought as she dabbed her cheek with a tissue.

When it was finally her turn to leave the plane, Regan rolled her bag up the aisle, said farewell to the flight attendants, and stepped onto the walkway with a feeling of freedom. And it was so nice that the air wasn't freezing. Starting to feel alive again, she passed through the gate area, inwardly sympathizing with the less-than-thrilled-looking passengers who were waiting to board the plane she had just gotten off. As she continued through the terminal, and headed toward the baggage area, she considered stopping at the ladies room but then decided against it. Too much trouble, she thought. But if she had, it might have saved her a lot of trouble. The actress she'd seen at JFK was busy primping in front of the mirror, spraying cologne, fluffing her hair, and reapplying makeup.

An elderly woman was waving her wet hands back and forth under a blower. "You look beautiful enough," she commented. "You must be meeting someone special."

"I am. He's very special. My new boyfriend will be waiting for me downstairs. I'm so excited . . ."

"Must be nice," the woman clucked.

Dean drove Cody to the curb outside the baggage claim area. "I feel like the hired help," he grunted. "I'm not going to be able to stay here. By the time Stella comes down, you have your big reunion, then collect her bags, they'll have chased me away. Either that or I'll have grown old. Call me when you're ready. In the meantime, I'll just keep circling the airport like an idiot."

"Thanks," Cody said. "Remember, Dean. Stella means a lot to both of us. With her in our movie—"

"I'll remember that when you two are holding hands and smooching in the back of my car. Now hurry up, keep your cap on, and pray that no one decides to take a picture of the grand reunion."

Cody got out of the car and walked through the automated doors to join the other people waiting to greet the arriving passengers. Most of them were drivers from car services. He tried to blend in. It was helpful that many of them were also wearing caps. I should have made a sign to hold up, he thought with amusement. On it he could have written Bunny, the name of Stella's character in their movie.

As he waited, he thought that this actually was kind of romantic. If only he didn't have to worry about being recognized by someone who knew Abigail.

A group of passengers started to come through. Most of them

didn't look happy. Traveling is stressful, Cody thought. Someday I want to have a private plane. If this movie is successful, I'll be on my way.

An attractive dark-haired woman was coming through the door. Something about her was familiar. Suddenly his knees almost buckled. She was another of Abigail's acquaintances. That private investigator who had lived across the hall. Oh my God! He turned away and with long strides, went out the door to the curb, crossed the roadway to the parking structure, and headed for a dark corner. What was her name? Abigail used to talk about her. Her name was Reilly. Regan Reilly. With trembling hands he pulled out his cell phone and called Dean.

"I'm on my way," Dean said as he answered the phone.

"No! Not yet! Abigail's former neighbor just got off a plane. Her name is Regan Reilly. She's a private investigator who moved to New York. Abigail was always going on about how smart she is, and said if we ever needed a private investigator, Regan was the one to call. Do you think Abigail could have asked her to come? The money I owe Abigail is due tomorrow. They'll track me down like a dog. And now Stella's around. She can't find out about Abigail or the IOU or—"

"Where is our star?" Dean interrupted.

"I was waiting for her when I saw Reilly. I got out of the terminal as fast as I could without attracting attention. You've got to be the one to greet Stella. Reilly never met you."

"You idiot. What if Abigail is picking her up? She'd recognize me. Although based on the night you met her, one of the longest nights of my life, she probably couldn't pick me out of a lineup."

"Then we'll have to keep Stella waiting until the coast is clear. We'll tell her we had car trouble."

"Oh great. We'll be late picking up the lead actress of our first movie. She'll love that. This has been some day. We lose an investor who gets cold feet at the last minute—"

"That old guy was really annoying," Cody snapped. "What a waste of our time. We sit there and have lunch with him, eat his lousy soup, then he bails on us. I still feel sick from all that sauerkraut."

"We'll never see him again," Dean said dismissively. "It looks like the one we have to worry about now is this Regan Reilly."

6

What luck, Regan thought, as her big black suitcase was the first one from her flight to come kerplunking down the chute. She grabbed it off the conveyor belt and moved out of the way. Her fellow passengers were jockeying for prime positions to spot and retrieve their bags. She reached in her pocket, pulled out her cell phone, and quickly dialed Abigail.

"Go outside. I'll be right there," Abigail said. "I'm in my white Honda Accord."

Regan wheeled her bags out the door, as usual surprised that no one these days ever seemed to check claim tickets, and walked to the curb. There was lots of activity as people hurried to load their bags into cars and taxis, spurred on by the announcements over the loudspeaker advising them to make it snappy. Some people really seem to enjoy slamming their trunks shut, Regan thought.

Within moments, Regan saw a white car that looked like it could be Abigail's heading her way. The driver was waving as the car pulled up. Abigail jumped out. "Hi!" she called as she ran around and gave Regan a hug. Abigail was wearing black jeans and a black shirt with loose sleeves. Regan immediately noticed the Ace bandage wrapped around her right arm.

"Abigail, you look great," Regan said.

"Thanks. You didn't have to say that. I look tired and stressed and I know it. Let's get your bags in the car."

"Don't you lift them!"

"I won't."

Abigail popped the trunk and got back into the driver's seat. A traffic officer was approaching them. "Move along!"

Thirty seconds later they were merging into the traffic leaving the airport. Abigail's eyes were darting back and forth from the rearview mirror to the side-view mirror as she navigated the car. "It's so crazy the way they rush people. How was your flight?"

Abigail is nervous, Regan thought. "It was fine. Pretty uneventful, which is good."

"I know you must be tired. I'll take you to the house where we're staying."

"Abigail, I was tired before but I feel better now. I don't think we should waste time. Why don't we go and get something to eat at the bar downtown where your friend spotted Cody? I'm hungry. A burger and a glass of wine would be great."

"Regan, are you sure?"

"Yes. I don't think there's a chance that Cody will be there, but I'd like to check it out. There had to be a reason he was downtown last night. Who is this friend of yours that saw him?"

"Her name is Lois Ackerman. I've known her for about a year. She's a hand model—nice but a real character. She's obsessed with keeping her hands beautiful and unblemished so she wears gloves all the time. I don't blame her. Those hands are worth a lot of money."

"Does she live downtown?" Regan asked.

"No. She worked on a commercial yesterday that was shot down there. It ran late. Afterward she went with a friend to get something to eat and that's when she saw him. I wish I'd been with her!"

"Did she try to go after him?"

"Not really, which just kills me. She said she started to but as soon as she stood up and ran outside, he disappeared. Believe me, Regan, she never runs anywhere. She moves slowly and deliberately so her hands don't bang into anything." Abigail groaned. "I shouldn't complain. Thanks to her I know he's around L.A. But Regan, that's not all; you wouldn't believe what's gone on in my life since you got on the plane."

"What?" Regan asked.

"This afternoon I heard from my lawyer. He says that the production company of the movie where I had the accident is balking about paying me. They don't want to involve their insurance company. They made an offer of ten thousand dollars. They must be kidding! I've been out of work for two months, I have to do therapy, and I could get arthritis, which could cut my career short. I don't even know when I'll be able to go back to work."

"Well, then stick to your guns," Regan advised.

"The only problem is that other producers might not want to hire me if I make too much of a fuss. They'll be afraid I might sue them one day. Word gets around. But this accident wasn't my fault. That piece of scaffolding just fell and knocked me over. They should be lucky it wasn't the lead actor who got hurt."

"It's so unfair," Regan said. "You shouldn't have to lose out because of their negligence."

"That isn't even the worst part of my day."

"There's more?"

"Regan, when I tell you this, you might want to go back to the airport."

Why did Jack have to go on that trip? Regan wondered.

"Abigail, don't be silly," she said with a slight laugh. "What happened?"

"I got a call from the police a few hours ago."

"Why?"

Abigail cleared her throat as they drove on the highway, headed for downtown. "I think it's good karma to try and do things for other people."

"It is," Regan said, wishing she'd get to the point.

"I feel like maybe if I do good deeds I'll stop being cursed."

Regan raised her eyebrows. "What goes around comes around," she muttered.

"You know how some people deliver meals to older people?"

"Yes."

"Well, after you moved I was so happy going out with Cody. I felt like the world was just wonderful. I decided I wanted to give back, so I started to cut elderly people's hair for free. I'd show up with my scissors. It just seemed like a nice thing to do for people on a limited income.

"It all started when I visited a friend of mine who works at an assisted living facility in Orange County. I offered to cut one of the old guy's hair who lived there. Then another man wanted a cut. So it started. I'd go down there every month and they'd be lined up. It was fun. One guy told me about a friend of his who lived up here and would be so grateful if I'd cut his hair. He lived alone and didn't have much money. So I called him. I cut his hair three months in a row. Then he started getting demanding. I went away on a shoot and he was annoyed at me because I couldn't come and cut his hair exactly when he wanted me."

"No good deed goes unpunished," Regan said.

"It gets worse."

"It does?"

"In September I got back into town and went over to his place right away. He lives in a modest little apartment in West Holly-wood. He sat in the chair and then asked me to go get the news-paper for him so he could read while I was cutting his hair. Can you believe it? He didn't even want to make conversation. So I go in the kitchen and he must have forgotten he left his broker-age statement on the counter. I know I shouldn't have, Regan, but I peeked at it. He was always acting like he had nothing. Well, my eyes almost popped out of my head. He had over a mil-lion dollars in his account! I cut his hair for free and he never offered me so much as a token of appreciation. I was furious but didn't say anything. When I was finished I told him it might be hard to come back again because I was so busy working all the time. I really needed the money. Hint hint."

"What did he say?"

"He started yelling at me and said I was selfish. I gave him a chance to offer to pay something and that's the way he acts? I wouldn't have even charged him that much! I'm happy to help people who need it, but it just kills me when people take advan-tage of your kindness."

"Abigail, why did the police call you?' "

"He was found dead today in his apartment. He fell back-wards and hit his head, but he hit it with such force, they're sure he was pushed."

"They don't think it was you, do they?" Regan asked aghast.

"I guess I must be what they call 'a person of interest.' The detective asked a bunch of questions, like, when was the last time I'd seen him, that kind of thing."

"How did they even know about you?"

"They found a picture of us in his nightstand. It was ripped in two. I was holding a pair of scissors over his head. We were laughing. I'd taken it with my cell phone and made a copy for him. I'd written my name and number on the back of it in black ink. He used to have it hanging on his refrigerator. At a later date he added, in red ink, "A witch with a bad temper."

"Oh boy," Regan said.

"Do you still want to go downtown?"

"Of course I do. With the way your day is going, I'm sure something exciting will happen."

7

Stella was standing outside the baggage area, clearly annoyed. Cody had not been there waiting for her, and he still hadn't arrived. She'd retrieved her suitcases and had dragged them out to the curb. The situation was so embarrassing. It was obvious that people recognized her and wondered why she was unescorted. She tried Cody's cell phone again.

"Stella!" he answered.

"Where are you?" she demanded. "This is completely ridiculous."

"We had so much trouble changing that flat tire you wouldn't believe it. Dean and I will have to include a scene like this in our next movie." He attempted to laugh, but to his ears it sounded fake.

"You still didn't answer me. Where are you?"

"Where are you?" was his reply.

"What kind of question is that? I'm here at the airport still waiting for you. If I had known it was going to take this long, I would have taken a taxi downtown."

"Did you get your luggage?"

"Yes. Of course I did. All the bags are off the flight and everyone else has gone on their merry way. When you called, you said changing that flat tire would only take a few minutes."

"I was more optimistic than I should have been. Dean and I are all thumbs when it comes to anything mechanical. But it's all done now. There's a brand-new tire on the car. We'll be there in just a few minutes."

"Okay. Hurry, would you?"

Cody hung up his cell phone. He and Dean were parked in the last row of the lot he'd scurried into after spotting Regan Reilly. It was a stone's throw from where Stella was standing. "The coast must be clear by now," he said. "We can't wait any longer."

Wordlessly Dean started the car, drove to the exit, and paid the parking fee. They went down the ramp, came around the bend, and saw the beautiful Stella glancing at her watch. She was wearing jeans, heels, and a very sexy top.

Dean sighed. "I could kill you. If I didn't want to make this movie so much, I would."

"The right girl is just around the corner for you," Cody answered. "I can feel it."

"I don't care what you feel. Get Stella in the car fast so we can get out of here."

Cody jumped out before Dean had fully stopped the car. "Baby!" he said as he gave Stella a hug.

"I thought you'd never get here," she said, pouting slightly.

Cody kissed her quickly. "I'm here now!"

Stella pulled off his cap and waved it in the air. "I've never seen you wearing something like this!"

Dean dashed out of the car and opened the trunk.

"Hi, Dean!" Stella called.

"Hi. I'll help load up your bags."

"Is there enough room?" Stella asked, as she started to walk to the back of the car. "If there's a dirty old tire in there, I don't want my suitcases to . . ."

Dean slammed the spotless trunk shut. "You're absolutely right. Let's get them in the backseat."

"I don't know whether they'll fit," Stella protested.

Five minutes later they were pulling out of the airport. Next to Dean on the front seat was one of Stella's enormous bags. They jammed the other into the backseat, leaving barely any room for Stella and Cody, which they didn't seem to mind.

"Cody, you don't seem like you just changed a tire," Stella said. "Your hands aren't dirty at all. I once did a scene in acting class that begins after my character's boyfriend changed a tire. My scene partner really got into it. He made himself all sweaty and put grease all over his hands."

"Dean keeps a carton of those hand wipes in the trunk," Cody replied quickly. "He's paranoid about germs."

Stella tapped Dean's shoulders. "That's a good way to be, Dean. There was a guy on the plane sneezing and coughing. He probably infected everybody."

Cody caressed Stella's shoulder. "You can't get sick for our movie."

"You'd better not," Dean said, trying to sound carefree. "You're our star. We have to take good care of you."

"You can start by feeding me. I'm hungry! Where should we go?" Stella asked. "We're in Hollywood! I want to live it up!"

"You do?" Cody asked with a hurt expression. "I thought Dean would just drop us off downtown and we'd have a quiet evening at the loft. I brought in some of your favorite food."

Stella's face fell, but she quickly recovered. "Okay then, honey. But tomorrow night let's go out and have fun. No one has to know we're dating. I'll be out having dinner with my two favorite directors, right, Dean?"

"Whatever you say, Stella."

"There's a new place I heard about in West Hollywood that's supposed to be really fun. It's called Uzi's. Why don't we go there?"

Cody felt sick. Tomorrow was Abigail's birthday. Ten to one she'd be out celebrating somewhere. Please don't let it be at Uzi's or wherever we end up, he prayed. Dean had been getting so upset lately, Cody didn't know what he might do if they ran into Abigail. For a little guy, he could be scary.

8

———◆———

Immediately after Mugs got off the phone with Walter, she went down to the senior center. Walter had told her that detectives working on the case wanted to talk to Nicky's friends. Five of the folks who knew Nicky from the center gathered to answer questions in the recreation room.

Walter had told Mugs that Nicky had been found on his kitchen floor. The resident manager had knocked on Nicky's back door because he left his clothes in the apartment building's only washing machine, and she didn't want to move them herself. When there was no answer, she peered in the window, saw Nicky on the floor, and ran to get help.

"Is anyone else coming?" one of the detectives asked Walter.

"I don't know. I left messages on people's answering machines . . ."

"Well, let's get started then."

It was established that Nicky had been at the center yesterday morning. Eighty-five years old, he was a man of few words. He'd had several heart attacks over the years and a couple of months ago had suffered one that Walter said "seemed to take the stuffing out of him."

Walter turned to Mugs, leaned toward her, and touched her arm. "Wouldn't you say so, Mugs?"

"Yes, I would. He was even quieter than usual," Mugs replied, instinctively leaning back.

"Do any of you have a key to his apartment?" Detective Vormbrock asked. He was the younger of the two cops, barrel-chested, with sandy hair and a moustache.

"Are you kidding?" Loretta Roberts answered dramatically, batting her clear blue eyes. "Nicky never would have let anyone have a key. He was always in control. He liked his privacy. I rang his bell once without calling first and he was not very hospitable."

"Why did you ring his bell?" Detective Nelson inquired. He was lean with olive skin and graying hair. His calm, practiced manner made it clear that he had been doing this line of questioning for years.

"Why did I ring his bell?" Loretta almost laughed. "Actually the problem was I *didn't* ring his bell, so to speak. I guess he didn't like me. I'd made a casserole for him after he had the last heart attack. He just took the casserole, mumbled a thank-you, and shut the door in my face. But I'm the type who doesn't hold a grudge, even though he gave me back the casserole dish with cheese still stuck to the sides."

The detectives' faces remained impassive. "So he wouldn't be someone who would let a stranger into his house?" Vormbrock asked, tapping his pen on his notepad.

"If he did, that would make me feel even worse," Loretta said with a wave of her hand.

After questioning everyone, the detectives learned that Nicky had worked at a flooring store for most of his life. He'd married when he was in his thirties, but his wife died five years later. He never married again. Several days a week he'd come by the center to play cards, but he wasn't interested in dancing or going to the movies with the group, even after knowing them all for ten years.

"He didn't talk about any problems he had with anybody?" Nelson asked.

Mugs shook her head. "No. He really kept to himself. But when people leave here, who knows what they're up to?"

Hilda, a blond-haired woman who taught the group how to square-dance, had been listening intently. "Detectives, are you collecting evidence?"

"Of course we are."

"Like what?"

"I'm sorry, ma'am. We can't really discuss that now," Vormbrock answered.

"I love all those crime shows," Hilda continued. "I can usually guess who the killer is before the detectives do."

Nelson smiled politely. "So no one knows of any plans that Nicky had for today?"

They all shook their heads no.

Walter clearly didn't want the excitement to end. "Did the manager of his building see any strangers in the vicinity?"

"As my partner said, at this point we really can't discuss much about the case but if any of you think of anything that might be helpful, please call us. We'll give you our cards. And if you don't mind, we would like your names and numbers. As we continue the investigation, we might have more questions for you." Nelson turned to the only man who hadn't said anything. "Sir, do you have anything to tell us about your friend Nicky?"

Leo had his cane resting in front of him, both arms wrapped around it. "Nah. Yesterday morning we played our favorite card game and I beat him. He seemed a little more upset than usual that he had to pay me two bucks. At the time I didn't think anything of it. He never liked to lose money. Now it makes me wonder what else might have been bothering him."

When Mugs went home, she didn't feel the same happy anticipation she would have normally felt about Ethel's pending visit. This could have happened to any one of us, she realized, as she checked the locks on her doors three times. I'm glad I'm going to live with Charley, she thought as she got into bed. It looks like Ethel is going to get a better deal on this apartment than she expected.

9

In her cozy apartment in Venice Beach, Lois was grateful to get in bed and under the covers. The television was on, turned to a news station. She reached for the tube of moisturizer on her nightstand, squeezed a dollop into her palm, and started to massage her hands. A burst of trumpets suddenly blared from Lois's cell phone, startling her for a moment. I've got to change that ring tone, she thought, as she glanced at the clock radio. It was 10:02. Who would be calling now? These days there was an unwritten rule about calling after ten. Text message, yes. Call, no.

"Hello."

"Lois, it's Abigail. Sorry I'm calling so late but I just picked up my friend Regan at the airport. We're in the car heading to Jimbo's. I thought if you were working late again tonight you might want to join us."

"Thanks, but I can't. I'm already in bed. I have to work early tomorrow."

"Just thought I'd check."

"Why are you going to Jimbo's? Cody will never go back there tonight."

"We know that. But I have Cody's picture and Regan wants

to show it to the staff. See if anyone recognizes him. Besides, we're both hungry."

"Hey, Ab, tomorrow's your birthday. I know your grandmother is coming in and you'll probably have dinner with her, but if you and Regan are going to be out looking for Cody tomorrow night, I'll gladly join you. I don't know what time I'll be free, but I can check in with you during the day."

"Thanks, Lois. Now you're sure it was Cody you saw last night, right?"

"Of course I'm sure."

"Okay, good. Regan was just asking me a bunch of questions about what happened when you saw him. You can probably tell you're on the speaker phone."

"Hi, Lois," Regan said.

"Hi, Regan. I've heard a lot about you."

"You, too. Abigail is so happy you saw Cody last night. I was just asking if there was any chance at all that it wasn't him. Abigail said it all happened so fast."

"It was definitely him. I only met Cody once, but I'm sure it was him. And what reason would anybody else have to run away when they saw me? That guy had a guilty conscience."

"There wasn't anyone with him?"

"No. That business partner of his was nowhere in sight, thank God. I hope I never see his face again. I couldn't stand that guy either. Both of them were so rude."

Abigail looked at Regan and rolled her eyes. Regan smiled. "What was Cody wearing?"

"Jeans, sneakers, a short-sleeved shirt. He was casually dressed, even a little rumpled."

"He looked rumpled?" Abigail asked.

"Yes."

"That's weird."

"Why?"

"Whenever we went out at night, he was always so put together. Believe it or not, he had a certain formality. He only wore sneakers during the day."

"I can assure you he didn't look formal," Lois scoffed. "As a matter of fact, his shirt looked too tight."

"Too tight? Is he putting on weight?"

"How would I know? But he looked really muscular. His biceps were big."

"Muscular?" Abigail repeated incredulously. "It was that noticeable?"

"Wasn't he in good shape last time you saw him?"

"He was. But no one would have looked at him in short sleeves and said 'Whoa, there goes a muscular man.' "

"I'm not calling that thief a muscleman, but his arms definitely looked brawny. I'm in the business, so that's something I'd notice. The night you met him he had on a jacket, so I didn't get a look at his arms. Not that I cared."

"Valentine's Day," Abigail said with disgust. "Can you believe it, Lo? We should have stayed home. Single girls who go out on Valentine's Day are asking for trouble. Jerks know that you wouldn't be out alone if you had someone in your life. If your boyfriend was out of town, you'd be sitting home eating the chocolates he sent you."

"Or admiring his roses," Lois said as she stared at a close-up on television of a woman's hand caressing a bottle of dishwashing liquid. "This Valentine's Day I'm staying home with the doors locked."

Abigail sighed. "Maybe he spent my money on a lifetime's gym membership."

"He looked healthy."

"That doesn't make me feel better."

"Sorry."

"All right, Lois. I'll talk to you tomorrow. Any recommendations on what we should order at Jimbo's?"

"Nothing. The food was lousy."

"Really?"

"Yes. I ordered a burger and it was incredibly greasy. The French fries were disgusting."

"What did your friend have?"

"He had a salad. It didn't look particularly inspiring."

"Who was your friend?" Regan interjected. "I wonder if he noticed anything about Cody that would be helpful."

"He was the male model from the shoot. But he was in the bathroom when Cody made his brief appearance."

"Oh," Regan answered. "Well, we'll see what we can find."

When she hung up, Lois flicked off the television and turned out the light. She was so tired, and tomorrow would be a long day. Abigail's birthday. Poor Abigail was in such a mess. I have to help her hunt down that jerk, Lois thought as she started to fall asleep. I just have to. He shouldn't be able to get away with what he'd done to her.

Or me.

10

When Regan and Abigail walked into Jimbo's it wasn't crowded, but there were enough people enjoying themselves to create a buzz. The place had the feeling of a relaxed neighborhood bar, unlike some of the more upscale restaurants that had sprung up since the renovation of downtown Los Angeles.

"Lois must have been sitting over there," Regan said, pointing to the tables by the window. "Let's grab a couple of seats at the bar."

"Hello, ladies," the bartender said with a smile as they sat down. "What can I get you?" he asked as he quickly ran a cloth over the counter in front of them. He looked young, with curly brown hair, a broad frame, and silver hoops of various sizes attached to his right ear.

They both ordered red wine.

"Coming right up."

A moment later Regan and Abigail clinked glasses. Abigail took a sip, turned, and looked past Regan toward the window. "I can't believe he was about to come in here last night. He was right outside! Ugh!"

Regan glanced around. "You know, Abigail, something tells

me if he was coming into a place like this by himself at that hour, he must be staying nearby."

"Maybe," Abigail said. "There are beautiful apartments around here. But Cody always wanted to be around West Hollywood, where more of the young film crowd hangs out. I think he'd come down here for fun sometimes but not to live."

Regan nodded. "You could be right. Can I see his picture?"

Abigail put down her glass. "It's right in my wallet, where it's been since he disappeared. I've been carrying it just in case, just in case I don't know what, maybe I'll run into someone who might have seen him somewhere." She reached into her bag. "It makes me sick," she said when she handed Regan the photo. "I took this picture of him when he came to visit me on the set in Montana. On my day off we drove around and stopped at a beautiful lake. I always kept this picture at my station in the hair and makeup trailer. What a joke."

Regan stared at the picture of a smiling Cody leaning back on a park bench, his arms outstretched, looking as if he didn't have a care in the world. In the background an expansive lake shimmered with the lights of a beautiful sunset. Clad in jeans and a white shirt, there was no denying he was handsome.

"Why would he bother visiting me on location if he didn't care about me?" Abigail asked. "This was only last August. He looks happy, doesn't he?"

"He does," Regan said. "And I'm sure he liked you. But people do stupid things after they borrow money. Who knows what he was getting himself into?"

" 'Neither a borrower nor a lender be,' my grandmother always said. I should have listened." Abigail took another sip of her drink. "I wonder what's going on with that stupid movie of his. I had no way of getting in touch with that idiot, Dean. And Cody wasn't allowed to tell me anything about the script because Dean was so afraid someone would steal their ideas. Give me a break!"

"Abigail, we're going to get up early tomorrow morning and hit the ground running," Regan said. She waved at the bartender who hurried over.

"Can we order some food?"

"Absolutely. Our specials are up on the blackboard. I also have menus."

"Before we look at them I have a question for you." Regan showed him Cody's picture. "We're looking for this guy. We heard he was headed here last night but never came in. Have you ever seen him? Maybe he was in here another night."

The bartender studied the photo. "No. Sorry. Did something happen to him?" he asked as he handed it back.

"Not exactly. He saw someone we know sitting at a window table and changed his mind about coming in."

"I wasn't here last night. You can ask the waiters about him, if you'd like."

"Thanks."

But none of the waiters had ever seen him. One of them, who had worked the night before, handed back the photo and said almost accusingly, "Did I hear you say another friend of yours was in here last night sitting by the window?"

Regan pointed. "A friend of Abigail's. We think that when he saw her, he changed his mind about coming in."

"Well, honey, I can see why." The waiter mimed pulling on a pair of gloves. "Was that your friend?" he asked Abigail.

"Yes, she always wears gloves."

He rolled his eyes. "She's very high-strung. I never heard someone complain so much about a burger. Please!"

Abigail made a face. "Sorry about that. She's not bad when you get to know her."

"I don't want to get to know her. That guy she was with must have gotten indigestion. But let me tell you something. For all her complaining, she cleaned her plate. I kept wishing she'd just take off those gloves and pick up her burger with her hands!"

"She's a hand model. She's afraid of taking off her gloves in public in case anything happens to them."

"I know. She told me as soon as I handed her the menu."

"The guy is a hand model, too," Regan said quickly.

"Really? At least he didn't wear gloves. Let me tell you something. I hope she never walks through this door again. Now if you'll excuse me, I have to go take care of my tables."

"Lois certainly makes an impression," Regan said with a smile. "I can't wait to meet her."

They ordered chicken wings and stuffed mushrooms and small bowls of chili. Everything was delicious.

Abigail was getting one last bite out of a chicken wing when she suddenly turned to Regan. "You don't think I'll have any more trouble with the police about the old man's murder, do you?"

Talk about a cause for indigestion, Regan thought. She slowly shook her head. "I don't think so. You haven't been there in months. He might have been mad at you but that doesn't make you a murderer."

"It was so strange when they were questioning me. I can't explain it."

"I'm sure it was difficult," Regan sympathized. "Being questioned about a homicide is not exactly idle chitchat."

Abigail insisted on paying the bill. They left the bar and drove around the neighborhood for a few minutes. It was nearly midnight on a Monday. All was quiet.

"Regan, you must be exhausted," Abigail said. "Let's head back."

"Which house are we staying in?"

"A little place that's owned by one of the actors who worked on the movie where I had the accident."

"Really?"

"He felt terrible when I was injured. Then I ran into him at the supermarket after I found out I had to move. He was leaving town for three months to do a movie in Europe and asked if I'd like to house-sit."

"He sounds like a nice guy," Regan said. "Those producers probably wouldn't be happy if they learned he's helping you out."

"Those producers would love nothing better than if I just disappeared."

Oh swell, Regan thought as they headed west on the highway. She looked at her watch. It was midnight. "Happy Birthday, Abigail."

Abigail rolled her eyes. "We'll see."

11

After Dean dropped the lovebirds off downtown, he drove straight to a twenty-four-hour gym in West Hollywood. Never had he felt such a burning need to work off a little steam and start building up his pecs. He had passed Nonstop Fitness a thousand times but had never darkened its doorstep. Now was the time. It had been an unbelievably horrible day, and Cody was driving him crazy. Not long ago, Dean had been handed a promotional one-day membership pass that he'd stuffed in his wallet. It was due to expire at the end of the month.

In the past, Dean had been too cheap to buy a health club membership. For the last couple of years he'd been in and out of town, working all over the country as a production assistant on movies. Most of his exercise consisted of scurrying around the set, following the orders of assistant directors who communicated only at the top of their lungs. Occasionally Dean jogged, but he had never been tempted to make a habit of it. The runner's high had thus far eluded him. Any slight feeling of well-being that he'd experienced was quickly forgotten. Finally tonight he realized that, if only for his sanity, he needed to hit the gym.

Nonstop Fitness was on Santa Monica Boulevard in the heart of West Hollywood. Not surprisingly, there were no parking spaces in front. Dean wasn't sure if the lot in the building was complimentary for customers of the health club, and he wasn't about to take any chances. Paying for parking tonight at the airport had already been irritating enough. Slowly he drove around the blocks near the gym, finally locating a small space on a darkened side street.

Curling his tongue as he concentrated, it took Dean three tries to parallel park his no-name sedan in the tight spot. He finally squeezed in without setting off anyone's car alarm. No wonder I don't do this kind of thing more often, he thought as he grabbed his bag and got out of the car. He opened the trunk that Stella thought contained a dirty flat tire, dropped the bag inside, and grabbed the pair of sneakers that he kept on hand in case he was out all day and his feet started to hurt. He might not use sneakers to exercise much, but they always felt comfortable. He pushed the trunk closed, and headed up the block. It felt good to walk in the cool, refreshing night air. One thing about Los Angeles, he thought, you can't beat the weather.

Inside the health club, a buff young man at the desk eyed him with a wary expression. "Can I see your membership card?" he asked.

"I have one of those free passes."

"May I have it, please?"

Dean handed it over. "Is there anyone who can show me how to use the weight machines?"

"At this hour?" the receptionist asked scornfully. "You must be kidding. We stay open late only out of consideration to our clients whose schedules preclude them from getting here dur-

ing normal hours. If you'd like to hire a trainer, I can call someone who will be here within thirty minutes."

"No thanks. I'll let them get their beauty sleep. I need to buy
a pair of shorts and a T-shirt."

Ten minutes later, after changing in the locker room, Dean
got in the elevator and went up one flight. When the door
opened onto the cavernous space, he was overwhelmed. Cardio
and weight machines were spread out as far as the eye could
see. His heart sank. I came here to relieve stress, he thought. I
must be crazy. The people working out on the machines looked
as if they'd been born there. He was reminded of the cool kids
in his class in high school who hung out perilously close to his
locker. He had always done his best to avoid them.

Dean headed for a row of treadmills that were unoccupied,
found one that didn't look too complicated, and climbed on. He
set the machine for a 45-minute program. He'd recently heard
that was how long you should exercise if you really wanted to
shake up those endorphins and feel better about your life. Let's
see if it makes a dent, he thought, as his feet started to move.

After a couple of minutes Dean was bored out of his mind. I
hate this, he thought. Just keep going, he told himself. One foot
in front of the other. He thought about the investors they had
to meet with tomorrow to close the deals. There were two of
them, and neither of them was particularly interested in the art
of filmmaking. One was a wealthy older man who loved the movies. When their film was ready, he planned to have a screening
for his friends followed by a big party.

"What I like is that your movie will only last thirty minutes,"
he'd said. "That's long enough. Any longer and my friends will
start to nod off."

The second potential investor was a young woman, recently

divorced from a very wealthy husband. She seemed bored with her life and spent most of her days shopping. She'd better not fall in love with Cody, Dean thought. I'll go out of my mind.

Then on Wednesday they'd be meeting with a retired couple who always wanted to be in show business. Their son had a house in Vermont and they planned to visit him at the end of January. If they invested, they wanted to spend some time on the set. They had already suggested that their grandchildren could be extras. Dear God, Dean had thought. He'd had no choice but to agree.

"You'll have to come by for lunch," he'd told them.

Now let's see if they all fork over the money, Dean worried as the treadmill started to move faster. It's only twenty-five thousand dollars each, but he and Cody needed every cent. The expenses just kept piling up. Now they'd have to entertain Stella for the next few days at restaurants that weren't known for their bargains.

Ten minutes passed. Twenty. Thirty. I can't believe I've made it this far, Dean complimented himself, as sweat dripped from his brow. Forty. The treadmill started the cool-down phase. Dean was elated. I did it, he thought. I did it. Forty-two. Forty-three. I'll lift some weights and then I'll head back to that dumpy apartment in Malibu. People thought if you had a Malibu address it meant something. They should see the hovel he had rented last year. I won't have to live there much longer, he promised himself. And tonight it won't bother me as much. Forty-five minutes. The treadmill stopped.

Dean sighed with relief. He turned and stepped off the machine. He felt light-headed but in a good way. Going for forty-five minutes does seem to make a big difference, he thought. He felt as if he was still moving. But wait . . . Something was wrong.

The whole building was shaking! People started to scream and run toward the doorways. Dean grabbed the handlebars of the treadmill but it was too late. He fell down on his behind.

Another earthquake had hit Los Angeles.

As people ran for cover, Dean put his head down and shielded it with his hands. It's all right, he thought sarcastically. Don't worry about me. I'll be all right. By the time the quake stopped, he realized that it hadn't lasted that long, maybe ten or fifteen seconds. He tried to pull himself up. Now my back hurts. Free pass or not I have to get out of here.

The locker room was crowded with people who just wanted to grab their stuff and get home. The quake had been relatively minor, but there was always the threat of aftershocks.

Dean didn't even take the time to change. Back out on the street, car alarms were blaring everywhere. Something told him to hurry. He started to jog but he couldn't. His back was too sore. Moving as quickly as he could, he made it down the block, turned the corner, and inhaled sharply. The trunk of his car was upright! Once or twice when he'd shut it, it didn't catch. He hadn't realized until he went to open it again. The jolt of the earthquake must have caused it to fly open! Pain or no pain, he tore across the street.

"Oh, no!" he yelped. "No!"

Not only did his trunk not contain a dirty flat tire, but there was no trace of his precious bag. The bag that contained all his important information about the movie.

Tuesday, January 13th

12

I always loved Laurel Canyon," Regan said as Abigail made a right turn off Sunset Boulevard and they started their ascent into the Hollywood Hills.

"Me, too," Abigail answered. "It has a special charm. You feel as if you're miles away from all the craziness, but you're not. And I love all these twists and turns," she said as she steered the car around one bend, then another, before making a right turn onto a narrow but steep lane. The car grunted as Abigail switched gears and pressed harder on the gas.

"We're gaining altitude," Regan commented.

"We sure are."

They traveled up the dark and secluded street, populated only by a handful of houses, following its curves until they reached the very end.

"Here we go," Abigail said as she pulled up to a high wooden gate, rolled down her window, and pressed in a security code. The gate swung open.

This won't be so bad, Regan thought.

But when they pulled in the driveway and made a slight turn to the right, the small dwelling perched on stilts reminded Regan of an overgrown tree house. Why would this place need a house sitter? she wondered. What it needs is a couple of hawks.

"Cute, huh?" Abigail asked.

Regan nodded. "Sure is."

"Brennan's done a lot of work on it. He's so handy. He built a deck off the back and made most of his own furniture."

"Great," Regan said. "I have to say, I've never known a guy like that."

"Me neither. I don't think my father has ever changed a lightbulb." Abigail pulled the car up to the carport, located smack under the house. They got out, retrieved Regan's bag, and walked to the driveway.

"What a view," Regan said as she looked out on the lights of the city.

"That's what this place is all about," Abigail said. "The view."

You got that right, Regan thought.

"Come on," Abigail directed. "We'll go in the back door. It's easier."

Regan rolled her suitcase as Abigail led the way up a stone path. Motion detectors had activated the security lights that partially illuminated the vertical backyard.

"That's some steep hill," Regan commented.

"I know. You'd have to be a nanny goat to get to the top."

When they reached the steps to the deck, Regan lifted up her suitcase and carried it.

"I wish I could help you with that."

"Abigail, don't worry."

They crossed the redwood deck and stopped at the back door. "I love to just sit here," Abigail said. "It's so peaceful and private. It makes me feel at one with nature." As she started to put the key in the lock, the earth started to rumble.

It only took a split second before the two of them realized what was happening. "Regan!" Abigail cried out, as an explosive noise filled their ears.

"Get away from the house!" Regan ordered, grabbing Abigail's good arm and linking hers through it. They moved a few steps from the back door as the earth shook. Regan reached for the railing of the deck and said, "Get down on your knees."

They both bent over, dropped to the ground, and covered their heads with their hands.

A few seconds later the movement stopped.

"Wait," Regan warned. "Let's just be sure . . ."

Nothing but an eerie silence filled the air.

"That wasn't so bad," Regan said optimistically.

"I've never been here during an earthquake," Abigail replied breathlessly.

"I was once—not a bad one. It felt just like this. Luckily there weren't any serious injuries."

"That's what counts, Regan," Abigail said. "With any luck my grandmother will now decide to postpone her trip."

"I admire your ability to immediately look on the bright side of things, Abigail."

"Thank you. You'll notice this did happen on my birthday."

"That thought ran through my head."

Abigail hesitated. "Do you think it's safe to go inside?"

"Is this house built to withstand earthquakes?" Regan asked.

"It just did, didn't it?"

"I guess you're right. Those stilts make me a little nervous."

"Brennan told me that everything is built to code. Nothing to worry about. This place is safe and sound."

"Okay then. Let's go."

Abigail unlocked the door, pushed it open, and turned on the lights. They stepped inside the kitchen and walked around.

To Regan, everything looked just as she would have guessed—wood walls, wood floors, logs on the ceiling, as if the whole place could have spontaneously grown out of the side of the canyon. There was even an earthy smell, which would take some getting used to. But it had a certain appeal. In the living room, a vase had fallen on the floor and broken in pieces. Various other objects had tumbled from their shelves.

"It doesn't look too bad. I'll clean up tomorrow," Abigail said. "Let me show you your room."

"We'll both clean up in the morning," Regan answered.

They went down a tiny hallway. Regan's room had a bed with a rough wooden headboard that looked like it might cause splinters. She was happy to see there was a television on the wooden dresser.

"Let's turn that on and see what they're saying about any possible aftershocks," Regan suggested.

Abigail flicked the remote control. As expected, news crews were being dispatched in all directions to survey the damage, but nothing major had been reported thus far. There were scattered power outages and reports of cans and bottles flying off the shelves at grocery stores. There had already been minor aftershocks but they were barely detectable.

The house phone rang. "Ten to one that's Brennan," Abigail said. "He's in Europe but word travels fast." She hurried down the hallway to the kitchen.

"Everything's fine," Regan heard her say. "A few things broke . . . No, your acting awards are still on the shelf."

Regan sat on the bed, staring at the TV coverage. I've got to muster the energy to open my suitcase, she thought as she watched reporters ask people how the earthquake made them feel. A moment later, Abigail was back. "Regan, I just thought of something."

"What?"

"I'm house-sitting two other places. The owners knew I wouldn't be staying there overnight but I'd better go check on them. There could be problems with the water or gas. You can stay here. I'll be back as soon as—"

"Abigail, you're not going alone. Of course I'll ride with you. Hey, where are those other houses, anyway?"

Abigail made a face. "One of them is in Malibu and the other is in the Valley."

We won't be back before dawn, Regan thought wearily, but kept a straight face. "That's okay," she said with a smile. "Give me a minute to freshen up."

"Regan, are you sure?"

"Of course I'm sure."

Regan's bathroom brought to mind a camping trip she'd gone on with the girl scouts many years ago. The sink and shower and toilet also looked like they somehow sprung from the wilderness. But there's nothing like running water to make you feel good, Regan thought as she splashed her face.

It was almost 1:00 when the two former neighbors ventured back out into the night. "Now, Regan," Abigail said as she double locked the door, "you can't tease me anymore when I talk about being cursed. Doesn't this prove it?"

"Abigail, I just hope that curse isn't contagious."

The two of them laughed as they walked down the stone path to the car, unaware of an intruder perched on the hillside.

13

It had taken Mugs a while to finally fall asleep. She dreamt that she was calling her sister to tell her what had happened to Nicky, but Charley's phone just rang and rang and rang. Then in her dream Mugs heard a knock at her door. When she answered it, Nicky was standing there. Mugs screamed and felt herself starting to sway. Her eyes flew open. She was swaying! The whole room was moving.

"An earthquake!" she gasped as she bolted out of bed. Oh no! Duck, cover, and hold. She knew the drill. Harry had drummed it into her head. If there were anyone more prepared for an earthquake than Harry had been, she'd like to meet them. Mugs grabbed the flashlight off her nightstand, and slipped her feet into the unattractive but sturdy "emergency" slippers she placed next to her bed every single night. Harry had bought them each a pair in case they had to "run like the dickens." She had never been able to put his slippers away after he died. They were still on the floor on his side of the bed.

Mugs ran to the doorway, crouched down, and covered her head and neck with her hands. Oh, Harry, she thought, remembering the last time an earthquake had struck late at night. They'd held on to each other in this very spot. Harry, I'm doing everything you taught me. I'm wearing these atrocious slippers. I just wish you were here . . .

Within seconds the shaking stopped. Mugs breathed a sigh of relief. "Thank God," she murmured.

Her phone immediately rang.

She flicked on the light and hurried back to her bed. "Hello."

"Mugs, it's Walter. Are you all right?"

"Yes. How were you able to call me so fast?"

"You're on my speed dial, Mugs. Not that it does me any good."

Mugs ignored him. "Thank you for checking on me. I do appreciate it."

"Do you want me to come over? I can be there in a few minutes"

"No."

"There might be aftershocks."

"I know. I've lived in California for a long time."

"It's been some day, huh?"

"It sure has. I was dreaming about Nicky."

"I wish you were dreaming about me."

Mugs rolled her eyes. The man was relentless. Another good reason to get out of town. "Walter, I think I'm moving to Florida to be with my sister."

"What?" Walter said. "Mugs, you're going to make me cry."

"Come on, Walter. Stop."

"My good buddy gets murdered. You're leaving town. As they say, old age ain't for sissies."

"I didn't know you and Nicky were so close."

"Maybe not close, but we were pals. Once in a while I'd go over there and watch a game with him. He didn't really get close to anyone."

"I wonder if the police have been able to get in touch with his niece."

"I don't know. I'll tell you one thing, she won't be shedding too many tears. I met her a few weeks ago when he was in the hospital. She was running back and forth from San Diego to look after him. Nicky was so ungrateful. He thought she was visiting just to be sure she was in his will. I got the feeling he wasn't planning on leaving her anything."

"If she's his only family then who would he leave his money to?"

"He said he was leaving it to the hospital in Long Beach that treated his wife. They said they'd name a room after her if he did."

"A room? How much money did he have?"

"My mother taught me it was impolite to ask people how much they had in the bank."

Mugs couldn't help but smile. "I was taught the same thing."

"Say, Mugs, what are you going to do about your apartment? It's not a good market for the seller these days. Shouldn't you wait until things turn around?"

"A friend of mine from high school, Ethel Feeney, is interested in buying it for her granddaughter. Ethel is flying out tomorrow to stay with me. We'll see if we can come to an agreement."

"Great timing. Negotiating a deal on your apartment the day after an earthquake."

"Thanks, Walter."

Walter laughed. "Does the granddaughter live here now?"

"Yes. She works as a hairdresser in films."

"What's her name?"

"She's too young for you, Walter."

"What are you talking about?" Walter protested. "I'm only interested in women my age. Unlike Nicky."

"What do you mean?"

"I'm just kidding. That small building he lived in has eight apartments. Except for the manager, who is in her sixties, all of the apartments are occupied by young women. One is better looking than the other. I'd tease him about it. He'd growl that he and his wife had lived there long before any of them were even born and why should he move."

"I hope one of these young women saw something that will be helpful to the investigation."

"Hey, it could be one of them who did him in. You never know."

"Well, whoever killed Nicky must have been someone he knew. He never would have let a stranger inside his apartment, and there was no sign of forced entry. That's what is so scary."

"You're right. I'm sure the detectives are questioning everyone. Now you're sure you don't want me to come over?"

"Positive. Good night, Walter." Mugs hung up the phone, and kicked off her emergency slippers. "I hope I won't have to wear these ever again," she muttered. Her terrycloth slippers with the embroidered snowflakes would be back in action tomorrow morning.

Mugs flicked on the television. Every channel had nonstop earthquake coverage, but all she could think about was Nicky. It was unbelievable that he had enough money to have a room at the hospital named after his wife. She thought of what Harry always used to say when someone asked him what the show he was working on was about.

"The story always boils down to love or money. My job is to make sure the lighting is good."

Surely Nicky wasn't killed by a jealous lover. That would be even more of a surprise than learning he had a lot of money.

But who could have done this to him?

And where were they now?

14

Detectives Vormbrock and Nelson had had a long day. They were back at the police station in West Hollywood, drinking coffee and reviewing their investigation. The body of Nicholas Tendril would be autopsied in the morning. There was little doubt that he had been shoved, causing him to fall back and hit his head against the kitchen wall, inches away from the clock. His body had crumpled to the floor.

"If he'd hit the clock and broken it, we might have the exact time of death," Vormbrock said wryly.

Nelson nodded. "Close but no cigar. Well, we know he hadn't been dead for that long when we arrived. Too bad his last meal was probably that soup he had on the stove. Boy did that smell up his whole apartment."

"Did it ever."

A bank receipt they'd found in Tendril's pocket indicated that he had withdrawn five thousand dollars in cash from his account at 11:10 A.M. that morning. It was not known what he did right after that. According to Gloria Carson, the resident manager of his building, who also lived on the ground floor, it was after 2:00 when she arrived home from her part-time job at a dermatologist's office. A while later, she went to do a load of laundry in the building's single washing machine located in a shed in the tiny backyard. But the machine was filled with men's clothes, which she recognized as Nicky's. Touching other people's laundry, clean or not, "gave her the creeps," so she knocked on his back door. There was no answer, so she peeked in the window, saw him on the floor at the far end of the kitchen, and thought he'd had another heart attack.

She'd run to her apartment, called 911, retrieved a master key, then hurried back and let herself in. When she first saw the body on the floor, she didn't get a look at his face. From her vantage point at the window, it had been blocked by the refrigerator. There was a series of wall cabinets at the far end of the room with a counter underneath that served as a desk. Nicky was lying between the refrigerator and the cabinets.

It was only when Carson let herself into the apartment and ran to his side that she saw all the blood around his head. She knelt down and cradled his head in her hands, but it was obvious he was dead. Agitated and hysterical, she ran to the front door when she heard the police, opening it with her now bloody hands. To say the least, her actions compromised the crime scene.

In the next few hours the detectives had searched the apartment for clues. They found the bank receipt, but there was no sign of the money in the apartment. They'd talked to a lot of people, but had no prime suspect.

"It's possible someone followed him home from the bank," Vormbrock said, staring at his notes.

"Maybe," Nelson answered. "But that was several hours before his time of death. He could have been tailed, and our perp was waiting for the right time to attack. The soup on the stove was still slightly warm, so I imagine he had been home for a while when he was killed. And that wash had already finished the cycle. But how would someone who followed him have gotten into the apartment? He was attacked in the kitchen, so it's not as if he answered the front door and someone pushed their way in. In that case, he would have been on the living room floor. The killer had to have been someone he knew."

"It's a safe bet that whoever killed him is now five thousand dollars richer." Vormbrock sighed. "Kill a guy for five grand?"

"But why was he withdrawing that money in the first place? His bank records show he never had made large cash withdrawals before." Nelson got up and poured himself another cup of coffee. "This Gloria Carson . . . It's interesting the way she doesn't want to touch his clean, albeit wet laundry, yet she doesn't mind getting his blood all over her hands. She didn't have to touch him."

"That is convenient, isn't it?"

"It is for someone who wants to appear innocent."

They reviewed the list of people they'd spoken to.

"And how about Abigail Feeney?"

Nelson shrugged. "This guy didn't have too many fans. She was one of the few people who went out of their way for him— she cut his hair for free. It looks like he could have used a haircut when he died. I don't know."

"She was injured on the job. She hired a lawyer to get money out of the production company. It's something to think about."

"I suppose it is." Nelson took a sip of his refreshed cup of coffee just as the ground started to shake. "Oh boy," he said as both men ran to the doorway.

15

Dean had decided he had no choice but to file a stolen-property report. He angrily slammed his trunk shut, then called 411 for the address of the West Hollywood police station. Our wonderful script is in the hands of a thief, he thought as he struggled to get out of the tight parking space. All that work. All my papers. Now it's Cody's turn to be furious with me. His name is on the script. He wouldn't want me to report the theft, but I have to. So what if his name shows up on the police blotter? It won't end up in the paper. We're not famous yet. No reporter is going to care. They only checked police blotters hoping to find something juicy involving celebrities.

At the station, the officer that Dean spoke with obviously had other things to worry about. His lack of interest in the theft was discouraging, to say the least.

"What was in the bag?" the officer asked blandly.

"Personal papers. A script that I wrote and will be producing and directing."

"Any cell phones, computers, cash?"

"No. Nothing like that. Believe me, those things would be easier to replace," Dean answered, his voice rising.

"Don't you have a copy of your script on a computer some-where?"

"Yes, I do. And I have e-mails saved that have a lot of the other information that's in the bag. But it's going to be so hard to duplicate and I'm very busy."

"We're busy here dealing with an earthquake."

"I know."

"Is the bag itself worth anything?"

"No," Dean answered, slightly embarrassed. "It's one of those nylon bags that are lightweight but sturdy—I wouldn't say it's valuable but it holds a lot of stuff . . . black with a zipper down the middle and a strap you can just throw over your shoulder."

The officer winced and held up his hand, the universal signal to just plain stop.

"Sorry," Dean said. "I guess I'm babbling. But this is very up-setting."

"Odds are the thief will realize there's nothing in there of any use to him and he'll toss it in a trash bin."

Dean moaned. "You think so?"

"I do. Let's get a report filled out. If anyone turns in the bag, we'll be sure to contact you."

"I guess I should drive around and check the garbage cans in the area."

"Look in the alleys, too."

"I wish I had a flashlight," Dean said, sounding pitiful. "At this hour there's no place open where I can buy one."

His expression never changing, the officer pulled open a drawer. "I've got an extra one here. Take it. Start yourself an earthquake preparedness kit."

"Thank you, sir. Thank you so much. If you'd like to come to a screening of the movie . . ."

"Don't worry about it."

When Dean exited the station, he drove back to the block where the bag had been stolen. All this aggravation because I wanted to get a little exercise, he thought, as he struggled again to park the car. Finally he got out and started down the block, pointing the flashlight in all directions.

Two minutes later the flashlight died. The batteries had gone kaput.

16

Abigail and Regan stopped at an all-night diner for coffee to go, then got on Sunset Boulevard and headed out to Malibu. It was a beautiful clear night and there was no traffic. Listening to the radio they learned that the earthquake had a magnitude of 5.2 and the epicenter was fifteen miles southeast of downtown Los Angeles. There were still no major injuries or damage reported. The biggest problem appeared to be the fact that cell phone service was down because of the overload, and land lines were jammed.

"That's amazing," Regan said. "Can you imagine if the earthquake had struck earlier? Most people who live farther east haven't even heard about the earthquake yet. They're all sleeping. I know I would have heard from Jack by now and certainly my parents. I didn't want to wake them, but now I can't anyway."

"I know, Regan. My parents are early risers. They get up with the cows. If the cell service comes back, I'll call them in an hour."

"You said Cody lived in Malibu with his writing partner, but you don't know where?"

Abigail shook her head. "No. I've driven out there so many

times in these past three months just to see if I'd spot one of them."

As they passed Bel Air, a gated community of mansions, Regan asked, "Who are the owners of the house you're watching in Malibu?"

"Okay," Abigail said, as if getting warmed up for a good story. "This couple is a hoot. They have tons of money on both sides and moved to Los Angeles from Long Island so they could meet celebrities."

"You're kidding."

"I'm not."

"Have they succeeded?"

"Oh, they've managed to meet people but it stops there. The two of them are so pushy. They buy tickets to all the expensive charity events to make the right connections, but I have the feeling they're not making many friends."

"How old are they?"

"In their late thirties. They have two teenaged kids. The whole family is off skiing in Switzerland this week and I'm keeping an eye on their house."

"Do they work?"

"She shops and he watches their money. He also takes acting classes." Abigail laughed. "I don't think Brad Pitt has anything to worry about."

"How did you meet them?" Regan asked.

"They rented out their house to a production company last year for a commercial shoot I worked on. The woman asked if I'd stay when the shoot was over and do her hair. She paid me a fortune. Now she has me come out to give the whole family haircuts when I'm in town. It's a great workday at the beach."

"That's nice," Regan said. "But why would they rent out their house if they have that much money?"

"They love showbiz and thought it would be a good way to meet actors. Now they're trying to sell the house but no one is interested."

"It's a tough time to try and sell a house."

"This house is a little more difficult to sell."

Uh-oh, Regan thought. "Why?" she asked.

"It's got a history."

"Abigail, what kind of history?"

"There was a murder-suicide in the house way back in the fifties . . . A guy came home and found his wife with another man. So he shot them and then turned the gun on himself."

Regan rubbed her forehead. "Abigail, if they have so much money, they probably had their choice of houses. Why did they pick that one?"

"I got the idea they thought it would bring them notoriety and provide an interesting entrée to the right people. They hired a publicist who was trying to set up interviews about living in the famous house. I think the local paper in Malibu wrote a small piece about them. That was it. People got turned off because it seemed they were begging for attention."

"Going there alone doesn't bother you?" Regan asked.

"No. I go there during the day. I told them I'd take the job, but there was no way I was sleeping over. They were fine with that. And, Regan, they're paying me a ridiculous amount of money. Right now, as you know, I really need it."

Abigail put on her left blinker and turned down a road leading toward the water. In another minute they were pulling up a long driveway to a rambling old house perched on a cliff overlooking the Pacific. This is no tree house, Regan thought.

"At least it's still standing," Abigail commented as she shut off the car.

"That it is," Regan said, taking in the sight of the beautiful old house that looked as though it should be in a movie. "Abigail, why do you think they want to sell it now? This is a magnificent spot, and if they didn't mind living here in the first place . . ."

"She wants to be closer to Beverly Hills, so she can shop. As you can see, it takes a little time to get out here."

They got out of the car and crunched across the gravel driveway. It would be so easy to shove someone over these cliffs, Regan thought as Abigail unlocked the massive front door and pushed it open. The alarm started to whine. She turned on the lights and quickly pressed in the security code on a panel by the door. The whining stopped and all was silent.

Regan looked across the large living room. Through the windows on the far wall she could see the Pacific Ocean sparkling in the moonlight. Abigail turned to Regan and wrinkled her nose. "It has a feeling of death in here, doesn't it?"

"Uh, I hadn't reached that conclusion yet," Regan said, imagining that the walls of this house certainly held great secrets. "When three people die like that in a house, I suppose it's never the same."

"It's not, Regan, I can assure you. This house is cursed. Just like me."

They walked through the rooms, which still contained much of the furniture that had been abandoned by the family of the husband and wife who died all those years ago. The furniture that the new residents had brought with them from New York was ultra modern. The effect was jarring. I'm sure people might want to come here out of curiosity, Regan thought. But from what this couple sounded like, not too many folks would want to come back.

The walls were covered with framed photos of an eager-looking couple standing with celebrities from A to Z. The two of them were smiling broadly in every picture. Some of the celebrities had a deer-in-the-headlights expression. The woman was a thin redhead, and the husband had a round face and light-brown hair. They weren't attractive or unattractive. Something about the look in their eyes gave Regan the feeling that they were strange. "I suppose these are your friends?" Regan asked Abigail.

"They're not really my friends, Regan. You're going to think that everyone I hang out with is a little nutty after hearing about Lois! But yes, it's them."

"What are their names?"

"Princess and Kingsley."

Now I've heard everything, Regan thought.

17

Before he retired for the night, Jack had ordered a wake-up call for 5:15. When the phone rang, he groaned and reached for the receiver. "Hello?"

A robotic voice answered. "This is your wake-up call . . ."

Jack hung up, jumped out of bed, and hurried into the shower. He'd found that the most painless way to get started this early was to get moving and under the hot water before he had a chance to think about how much he'd rather stay in bed.

The shower did the trick. He was slowly coming to life. When the hotel room's doorbell rang at 5:30, he had just finished shaving. The previous night he'd filled out the breakfast menu and hung it outside his door. At the seminars yesterday, the breakfast food consisted of trays of pastries that tasted like cardboard. Today Jack wanted to have a healthy start with cereal and fruit and juice, then catch up on messages from the office before heading down to the meetings, which started at 7 A.M.

Wearing the hotel bathrobe, Jack hurried to the door and opened it.

"Good morning," a young man holding a tray said cheerfully. "May I come in?"

"Yes," Jack replied, wondering if anyone who'd ordered up breakfast ever said no.

"Shall I pour you your first cup of coffee?" the waiter asked as he set the tray on the desk.

"Sure. While you're doing that, I'll sign the check."

Their tasks completed, the waiter thanked Jack. "And please call room service when you're finished with your tray," he requested as he went out the door.

Jack reached for the coffee cup with his right hand, and flicked on the remote control of the television with his left. When the screen lit up, the cup almost fell out of his hand.

The headline EARTHQUAKE HITS LOS ANGELES assaulted his senses.

"Regan!" Jack said, hurrying to grab his cell phone, which was plugged in by the bed. He quickly pressed in her speed dial number but was rewarded with the news that all circuits were busy. He turned up the volume on the television. An anchor was standing in front of the Staples Center in downtown Los Angeles.

"The quake occurred roughly two hours ago. So far there are no reports of major injuries but we've heard that people have gone to the emergency rooms with broken bones . . ."

Jack's head was telling him that Regan was okay, but his body wasn't believing it. He felt as though he was going to pass out. Why haven't I heard from her? The tray of healthy breakfast food suddenly seemed ridiculous and unimportant. His cell phone rang. Fearing the worst, he grabbed it. Regan's name was on the caller ID.

"Regan?" he asked anxiously, a catch in his throat. "Is that you? Are you okay?"

"Yes, Jack, I'm fine. I guess you heard. I didn't want to call you when it happened and wake you up."

At the sound of her voice, Jack closed his eyes, relief flooding him. "Regan, sweetie, do me a favor. Next time, wake me up."

"I'm sorry, Jack. I knew you were tired . . ."

"Now I feel exhausted," Jack said with a slight laugh. "I turned on the television and they're talking about an earthquake in California. I tried to call you but couldn't get through. I almost had a heart attack . . ."

"I really am sorry," Regan said. "Maybe I'd better call my parents."

"You think? Oh, Regan, you are funny. I wish you'd stayed home and tended to that new storage unit of yours."

Regan laughed. "I've got plenty of time for that. Okay, I guess I'd better give Luke and Nora a buzz. I love you."

"I love you, too. Tell me, how's it going?"

"I think you've had enough excitement for today, Jack."

"What do you mean?"

"I'm kidding."

"How's Abigail?"

"She's fine."

"Really?"

"No. As I told you, she's got a lot on her plate. But get this: yesterday when I was on my way out here, she was questioned about the murder of an old man whose hair she used to cut for free. I'm telling you, Jack. I'm starting to believe that girl really is cursed."

18

While Regan was outside calling Jack, Abigail walked through Princess's house one more time to make sure it was secured. She then went into the kitchen, where the celebrities in the framed pictures were limited to those famous for the preparation or serving of food. Abigail picked up the phone on the wall and pressed the speed dial for Princess's international cell phone. The connection was made and the phone started to ring in that funny way that reminds you you're not calling someone down the block.

Princess's voice mail picked up. "Hello, this is Princess! I'm skiing in the Alps at this very moment. Isn't that fabulous? Can't wait to tell you all about it. Please leave a message. If you need immediate assistance with anything at all, please don't hesitate to call our Gal Friday, Abigail Feeney, and she'd be happy to assist you. Her number is . . ."

"What the . . ." Abigail muttered. At the sound of the beep she began, "Hi, Princess, it's Abigail. We had an earthquake here in Los Angeles but I'm at your house and everything is fine. Have fun." Abigail hung up the phone. Well I guess I shouldn't complain, she thought. They are paying me well. But "Gal Friday"?

Abigail looked at her watch. It was 2:35 A.M. Which meant it was the crack of dawn in Grandma Ethel's little farmhouse in Indiana. Time to call her and see if I can fend her off, Abigail thought. She pulled her cell phone out of her pocket, braced herself, and dialed the number.

Ethel Feeney had been up for an hour. She'd already fed the chickens and drank two mugs of boiled water with lemon. When the phone rang, she was on the floor doing leg lifts. Her flight wasn't until later in the day and would get her into Los Angeles around 5:00 P.M. She could barely contain her excitement.

"Grandma, how are you?"

"Thrilled as can be, Abigail. I'm going to get to see you today. Happy Birthday! What are you doing up? It must be the middle of the night in Los Angeles."

"Grandma, I hate to tell you this, but we had an earthquake."

"Was it bad?"

"No, not too bad. But it was an earthquake. I don't know whether you might want to change your mind about the trip."

"Fiddlesticks! I'm sorry I missed it. I've survived tornadoes, floods, hurricanes, and fifty-three years living with your grandfather. I'm happy to say I've had almost every experience. Before I die, I want to be able to say I've experienced it all."

"Okay then, I just wanted to make sure . . . Some people think it might not be a good time to invest in real estate."

"It's a great time. I'll get Mugs to lower the price."

"Wonderful, Grandma. I'll see you later at the airport. I'll be waiting where you come through to baggage claim."

"Super! Now listen, honey, if you'd like to invite a few of your friends to dinner tonight to celebrate your birthday, please do. We'll have a ball!"

"Thanks, Grandma! You're the best." Abigail hung up. I'm doomed, she thought. Doomed.

19

After Dean's flashlight died, he drove to a 7-Eleven to buy batteries. There was a long line of people stocking up on bottled water. Where did you people come from? he wanted to shout. It's the middle of the night! Go home and get some sleep!

By the time he made it to the checkout, Dean was ready to burst. When he placed his batteries on the counter, the cashier ignored him, having decided that it was a good time to replenish the quarters in his drawer. Dean could barely contain himself but waited silently as the cashier banged the roll of coins against the counter, broke the paper seal, and slowly dropped the coins into the register.

When Dean got back in his car, he felt like a madman. He drove back to the street where his bag had been stolen, parked his car there for the third time that night, and resumed his search. Up one block and down the next. He poked through every trash can in West Hollywood, and searched every dark alley, risking life and limb. There was no sign of his beloved black bag.

At one point he sat down on a curb and almost started to cry. But a weird-looking guy walking a big German shepherd started coming down the block. Dean jumped up and headed back to his car.

There's no use, he thought. I'll never find it. Completely dejected, he headed home to Malibu. The same thought kept running through his head.

Cody is going to kill me.

20

When Regan hung up with Jack, she called the Breakers Hotel in Palm Beach and was put through to her parents' suite.

"Hello," Nora answered drowsily.

Oh good, Regan thought. My mother obviously hasn't lost any sleep worrying about me. Jack's the only one I have to feel guilty about. "Mom, hi, it's me."

"Regan, hi. How are you?"

"I'm fine. There was an earthquake out here but it wasn't too bad. I just didn't want you to find out about it on the news. The phone lines have been tied up until now."

There was silence at the other end of the phone.

"Mom?" Regan said. She could hear Nora's even breathing and thought she detected a slight snore emanating from her father. "Mom?"

"Hmmm?"

"Go back to sleep."

"Okay, dear. Good to talk to you. Love you."

The phone clicked in Regan's ear. Well, what do you know, she thought. Wait until Jack hears about this. She smiled. Life is full of surprises.

Abigail came out the front door, locked it, and walked to the car where Regan was standing. "Everything okay?"

"Fine," Regan answered. "We're all set?"

"Yes. I just called my grandmother. She's raring to go. The earthquake didn't bother her one bit."

"It didn't seem to bother my mother either."

"Oh God, Regan, it's almost three o'clock in the morning. My grandmother is going to be here in fourteen hours. I'm starting to panic. I've got to get that money back from Cody!"

21

Cody, I'm telling you I'm too scared to stay here. We're on the fourteenth floor! If another earthquake strikes, we're dead," Stella said.

The two of them were sitting under a doorway in the loft. Stella had been too petrified to move from the floor even though the earthquake occurred over two hours ago. At first it had been romantic the way they'd huddled together. Cody had gotten up only once to turn on the television. But now the initial thrill had worn off, and the reality that another earthquake could happen at any time was settling into Stella's brain.

"Baby," Cody said, doing his best to sound soothing, "this building is strong. I'm telling you."

"No it's not. This is an old building and we're high up. We could never run outside in time."

Cody rubbed her hands. "I'll protect you."

"Don't be ridiculous. I want to get out of here. What about going to Dean's apartment? Didn't you used to live with him?"

Cody almost choked. Living with Dean consisted of crashing on a futon next to Dean's bed in a flea-bitten hovel by the beach. He'd never let Abigail come near the place even though she kept asking to. "I did live with him for a while a couple years ago. But we can't go there now because he's having it painted. The fumes are really bad. You wouldn't be comfortable, and that's all I care about." He gave her a little kiss.

"I can't wait to see it," Stella said quietly. "How great to have a view of the ocean. It's too bad you don't have your apartment anymore. Didn't you say that that was on the ground floor? We'd be safer there now."

"It was," Cody lied, caressing Stella's cheek. "But when a building gets sold it gets sold. I had to get out. Now I'm glad I didn't jump into buying a house because I know that whatever place I buy, it has to be a place you love." He rubbed the side of her face. "You okay now?" he asked softly.

"No, Cody, I'm not. Let's get our stuff together and leave."

Cody's heart started pounding. "Where do you want to go?"

"How about the Beverly Hills Hotel? I always dreamed about staying in one of their cottages."

Oh my God, Cody thought. That was one of the most expensive hotels in town. Never mind a room, but a cottage? He and Dean were watching every penny. He'd used the last of Abigail's money splurging on presents for Stella and her family at Christmastime. The hotel might reject his credit card! "Stella," he said in his most tender voice. He put his arms around her and pulled her close. "Why don't you just try going to sleep? You'll feel better in the morning."

Stella pushed him away and stood up. "You don't get it, do you? You don't care how I feel at all! I'm a nervous wreck. How can you be my boyfriend, never mind direct me in a film? Call me a cab. I'm leaving."

Cody jumped to his feet. "I'm sorry, Stella, I didn't realize. I'm going with you. We're going to the Beverly Hills Hotel together this minute. Right this minute. Let me call Dean."

Stella was already packing her bag. "Why do you have to call Dean? He's all the way in Malibu."

"He'll want to drive us."

"That's crazy. I don't want to wait that long. There has to be a cab or a car service."

"Okay. Let me call the hotel and make a reservation."

"You can do that from the cab."

"What if they're booked?"

"Then we'll call someplace else. I'm not staying here another second! I'm having an anxiety attack. I will never forget the way the room shook . . ." She stifled a sob. "My career is just beginning. I have so much to look forward to . . ." She hurried past him to the bathroom and slammed the door.

Cody grabbed his phone and ran to the other side of the loft to call Dean. Surprisingly he answered on the first ring.

"Cody?"

"Dean! You're not going to believe it."

"What?"

"Stella insists on getting out of here. The earthquake really scared her. She wants to go to the Beverly Hills Hotel and stay in a cottage."

"The Beverly Hills Hotel? We can't afford that!"

"I know. But we have to. She threatened to leave without me."

Dean pulled his car to the side of the road. Otherwise he would have lost control. "Well, go ahead then. What are you calling me for?"

"I'm a little worried about my credit card. If I request a cottage for three or four nights, they might check my limit. I overextended myself at Christmas and I'm just afraid—"

"What do you want me to do?"

"Could you go there now and book a cottage? Pick up some flowers along the way and wait in the lobby to greet us. It will make Stella realize how much her two directors are only concerned about her safety and well-being."

"Where am I supposed to get flowers at three in the morning?"

"I don't know!" Cody whispered. "Find a rose in someone's yard. I'm telling you, it will be a nice gesture."

"Not for the person who owns the yard."

"Come on, Dean! This is what directors do for their leading ladies."

"She's more your leading lady than mine," Dean snapped. "All right, Cody. Now it's my turn to give you bad news."

"What?"

"My bag got stolen out of my car tonight."

"That bag with everything in it?"

"Yes. I reported it to the police."

"You did?"

"I had to. Otherwise I might never get it back."

Cody gasped. "She's coming out of the bathroom! We'll see you there." He hung up.

Well that's out of the way, Dean thought. He put his car in drive, pulled out, and did a U-turn.

My mother always told me I was crazy to go into showbiz.

22

The third home that Abigail was house-sitting was in the town of Burbank, located on the other side of Laurel Canyon in an area known as "The Valley." Numerous media and entertainment companies had their headquarters in Burbank, and many of the people who worked in those companies made it their home as well.

"I hesitate to ask whose house we're going to now," Regan joked, trying to lighten the mood. It was clear that Abigail was getting more and more nervous about the impending arrival of Grandma Feeney.

Abigail smiled. "I swear, Regan, this older lady is normal. Her name is Olive Keecher, and she's very interesting."

"You make it sound like I'm going to meet her."

"I'd love for you to meet her. And if you need any clothes tailored, Olive's the one to do it. She has a little business she operates out of her house. Nothing official. For more than fifty years, Olive worked in the costume departments of different studios."

"How do you know her?" Regan asked.

"The same way I knew old Nicky, may he rest in peace. I was down at the assisted living center doing haircuts, and Olive was visiting a friend. We exchanged cards. Now I cut her hair and she sews my buttons. I'm hopeless with a needle and thread. When she visits her daughter in Atlanta every other month, I water her plants and collect her mail. I was already there today, so all I have to do is make sure the earthquake didn't do any major damage."

Abigail turned down a quiet tree-lined residential block. "It's the third house on the right." She pulled the car into the driveway.

Regan looked at the small, attractive white house. "Was anyone murdered here?"

"Regan!"

"Just asking," Regan said as she got out of the car.

Inside the cozy living room, there were a few knickknacks scattered on the carpeted floor. "That's not too bad," Abigail noted, as she placed them back on the shelves. "As you'll see, Olive goes a little crazy tying ribbons around her cabinets and drawers when she leaves town. She lost all her dishes in a big earthquake years ago."

They checked Olive's bedroom and found everything in place. A second bedroom had been transformed into Olive's workroom. A sewing machine faced the window. Countless spools of thread were lined up on a shelf above. Bolts of fabric were propped against a wall. A mannequin was standing upright in the corner.

"I'm in awe," Regan said. "I can't sew to save my life."

Abigail pointed. "Those framed posters are of movies she worked on. Some of them were made so long ago. Olive has great stories about the stars from way back."

Regan walked over to a shelf and picked up a form resembling a woman's hand. "Look at this."

"Once in a while Olive makes gloves. I tried to get Lois over here but she's so busy all the time."

Regan raised an eyebrow. "I don't know, Abigail. How much do you like this woman Olive?"

Abigail laughed. "Lois is not that bad. I wonder how she reacted to the earthquake. I have to call her."

They checked the rest of the house, locked up, and headed back to Laurel Canyon. When Regan got in bed, she was so tired she didn't even worry about whether the headboard might give her splinters. I can't believe I started this day by renting a storage unit, she thought. And I'm ending it in a tree house.

She was about to drift off to sleep when her cell phone rang. It was her mother.

"Regan! Are you all right?"

"Yes."

"What about the earthquake?"

"Mom, I called you. Don't you remember?"

"Vaguely. But now I'm awake! We're watching the reports on the news. I'm sorry if I didn't seem concerned when you called."

"I know you're concerned," Regan said. "Let me call you back in a few hours. I'm just falling asleep now."

"You haven't found the boyfriend yet?"

"No. We've been busy."

"Good luck."

"Believe me, Mom, we'll need it."

23

Regan awoke to the enticing scent of freshly brewed coffee. When she opened her eyes, the sight of the logs above the bed brought her to full consciousness. Oh yes, she thought. Here I am. At one with nature in all its glory. All was still and peaceful and eerily quiet in the dusky room. Overhanging trees outside the window prevented much light from filtering through. If I hear cock-a-doodle-doo the scene will be complete, Regan thought as she pulled the blanket around her chin and turned on her side. The air was chilly, as it often is in the early morning in Los Angeles.

Regan glanced at the clock radio next to the bed. 7:17 A.M. I slept like a rock but not for very long, she thought. This room is like a cave. If it weren't for that coffee, I don't know when I might have woken up. She dragged herself out of bed, put on a pair of sweats, and a few minutes later walked out to the kitchen.

There was no sign of Abigail. Regan glanced out the window and saw her sitting on the deck, a cup of coffee on the table in front of her. She was wearing a bathrobe, and staring off into the vertical backyard. Regan opened the back door. "Good morning, Abigail," she called.

Abigail turned. "Regan, I was hoping you'd sleep in a little bit."

"I don't want to." Regan held up her notebook. "We've got work to do."

"Let me get you some coffee," Abigail offered as she got up. "We can sit inside. It's a little brisk out here."

"I don't mind. Besides, I'll be going back to cold weather in New York and won't be able to dine alfresco for quite a while."

"Great. Would you like toast? Yesterday I bought country bread from the Laurel Canyon general store. It's delicious."

"Sure."

A few minutes later they were sitting down to breakfast at a round patio table, which, naturally, Brennan had carved himself.

"This is such a peaceful spot," Regan remarked as she looked around, "and it feels so isolated. You'd never know that we're a two-minute drive from a traffic jam."

"It would be a good place for your mother to write," Abigail said as she spread raspberry jam on her toast.

"It would," Regan said agreeably, amused at the thought of her mother contending with Brennan's primitive bathroom. She reached for a piece of melon. "Oh, Abigail, once again I'd like to wish you a happy birthday."

Abigail shook her head. "No matter how it turns out, this will be one birthday I'll never forget."

"Hopefully for good reasons." Regan opened her notebook and picked up her pen. "Okay, Abigail, let's get started by going over the facts. Before Cody suddenly disappeared, they were trying to get the movie going. But your money wasn't an investment in the movie, right?"

"Right. Cody didn't want that. He didn't want me to risk any money and neither did I. He said it was strictly an IOU."

"Makes sense," Regan said. "But what did he need it for then?"

"He said he needed to have money in his account in case they had to apply for loans, or if any of the investors wanted to check on his financial status or Dean's. He promised he wasn't going to spend one cent of my money, he just needed to have it in his bank account. I was so stupid. What was I thinking?"

"Don't beat yourself up now, Abigail. What's done is done."

"Okay."

"Did Cody have any jobs in the time you were with him?"

"No. It's so embarrassing. He was working on the script and then lining up investors. That's what he and Dean had devoted the year to."

"How could he afford that?"

"Obviously he couldn't. That's why he borrowed money from me." Abigail threw down her napkin. "What if it's all gone?"

"Abigail, don't think about that now. Next question. Cody's writing partner, Dean. You don't know his last name?"

Abigail shook her head. "No. We never did anything together, and Cody always came to my place. I think Dean never got over the night we met and he was stuck with Lois."

"You never went to their place?"

"No. Cody said it was a bachelor pad in the worst sense. He insisted my apartment was a much nicer place to hang out, and said it was so soothing for him." Abigail clenched her knuckles and bit down on them. "Aaaagh." She looked over at Regan. "Sorry."

"It's okay. You're sure the 'bachelor pad' was in Malibu?"

"That's what he said. For all I know they could have been living in a storage unit. People have tried that out here."

"I rented a storage unit in New York yesterday."

"You're kidding."

"I'm not. We'll talk about that later. Cody didn't tell you the title of their movie?"

"It didn't have a title yet. Dean is such a nerd. He said Woody Allen's movies were often untitled while they were in production, and what was good enough for Woody Allen was good enough for them. Dean was trying to create a mystique. As I look back, I can't believe I didn't find that pathetic."

"Do you have any idea what the movie was about?"

"No. When I lent Cody the money, he promised he'd let me read the script that weekend. They'd just finished the umpteenth draft and he was finally ready to hear my opinion. Then he disappeared."

"But he said he'd pay you back on your birthday."

"Yes. He said they wanted to start filming the movie in January and by then all the funding had to be in place, so he wouldn't have to worry about keeping a big balance in his account."

"Do you know where they wanted to film?"

"No. The movie could be set in Alaska, for all I know."

"If Cody was in Los Angeles the other night, then there's a chance they're filming it here now. And if they are, there has to be some paper trail we could follow. They would have had to get permits, things like that. We can check and see if Cody's name is listed on any of the movies in production."

"Okay," Abigail said hesitantly, afraid to get too hopeful. "But I've been asking around and nobody I know has heard anything about a project involving Cody."

"Abigail, you know there are numerous movies in production out here. That's what this town is about. No one could possibly be aware of them all."

"I hope you're right, Regan."

"What about Cody's family? Did you ever meet them?"

"No. His parents are divorced and he's like you, an only child."

"Not too much like me, I hope."

"He's not like you at all, Regan."

"Thanks. Where did he grow up?"

"All over. He said he hated moving around so much when he was a kid. His father could never keep a job. Then his parents divorced when he was a teenager. Shuttling back and forth between them for the next two or three years was no fun. Once he was eighteen he went to college and was more or less on his own. His mother married a wealthy guy, and they were always traveling. I get the feeling she's a real glamour-puss. Cody's father was always running around with younger women. I have absolutely no idea how to find them, and I'm sure they wouldn't want to hear from me anyway." Abigail sighed. "Cody said he always wanted stability and was so happy to have found it with me. Doesn't that make you sick?"

"In his own way, he might have meant it," Regan said with a shrug.

"Don't try and make me feel better. He's a liar and a thief and I want my money back."

Regan stood. "I'll get out my laptop. Let's see what we can find. I've got the feeling Cody Castle's name has to be attached to something going on in this town."

"Better not be bankruptcy court," Abigail muttered. She looked at her watch. "Nine hours and counting until Grandma Ethel's plane touches the ground."

24

Dean was exhausted when his alarm went off early Tuesday morning. He hadn't gotten more than two hours of sleep. The night before, he'd driven to Beverly Gardens Park at the corner of Santa Monica and Wilshire and risked arrest by picking a rose from one of its famous bushes. Then he'd driven to the Beverly Hills Hotel and told the front desk clerk that he'd like to book one of the cottages for friends who would be arriving momentarily.

"You mean a bungalow?" the clerk had asked disdainfully.

"Cottage, bungalow, whatever you want to call it," Dean had snapped. "Give me the one Greta Garbo stayed in, if you have it. My friends are like her. They crave their privacy."

"They're called bungalows, my good man. We have one left."

"I'll take it." Dean had handed over his credit card, then sat in the gorgeously appointed lobby and waited for the arrival of Romeo and Juliet. I can't believe this, he thought. I'll go home to the dump while Cody stays in the lap of luxury for the next three days, pretending he's actually got a dime in his pocket. I just hope none of his acquaintances from the jailhouse happen by.

When the twosome arrived, Stella acted as though she were the only person in Los Angeles who'd experienced the earthquake. "Dean," she'd cried, giving him a hug. "You're here! It was all so scary."

Dean handed her the rose. "Cody called and told me you'd feel better if you stayed at this beautiful hotel. I jumped in the car and came straight here to make sure things went smoothly. Luckily I was able to book you two the last bungalow." He laughed and lowered his voice. "Whatever you do, don't call it a cottage."

Stella laughed and sniffed the rose.

"I just wanted to make sure that you feel secure," Dean continued.

"I do now."

Dean turned to Cody. "Here are the keys to the bungalow. We have a meeting tomorrow morning. I'll pick you up at 9:30."

"Should I come with you?" Stella asked.

"No," Dean answered quickly. "One of our major investors just wants to go over a few points in our agreement."

"But wouldn't an investor like to meet the star?"

"Let's keep the mystery," Dean suggested. "You relax and rest up for the film. I see the bellman is waiting to escort you. Run along, kids," he said with a laugh.

"Thanks, man," Cody said with a wave. "Appreciate all you've done."

Dean darted out of the lobby, paid the outrageous parking fee, tipped the valet, and drove off into the night. For a fleeting moment he'd been tempted to search the garbage cans in West Hollywood one last time, but decided enough was enough. He'd go home and lay down his weary head.

Now it was 8:30 A.M. and he was printing out scripts. He'd frantically gone through e-mails to find the addresses of the people they were meeting with today. At least I didn't lose my computer, he thought. That would have been the end.

While the printer was whirring, Dean turned on the television. A reporter was standing in front of Nicky Tendril's apartment building.

"Eighty-five-year-old Nicholas Tendril was found murdered yesterday. His attacker pushed him against a wall in his apartment. Tendril died immediately of head injuries. Police are asking anyone with any information whatsoever to please call the hotline . . ."

Oh no, Dean thought, his head swimming. No. He couldn't have . . .

25

Kaitlyn Cusamano had worked as activities director at the Orange Grove Assisted Living Facility for nearly two years. Besides the usual bridge games and bingo, she managed to arrange, on a limited budget, activities such as dance lessons, painting sessions, photography classes, piano recitals, and speakers who would be of interest to the seniors. The job was challenging and rewarding. It gave Kaitlyn great satisfaction to witness people who were faced with the burdens of old age find pleasure in the diversions she worked so hard to offer them.

This morning she'd left the small apartment she shared with a roommate earlier than usual. By 8:15 she was parking her car near the main entrance of the facility. She wasn't due until 9:00, but it was her first day back from vacation, and she was sure some of the residents would be out of sorts after the earthquake last night. Many of them liked to stop by her office in between scheduled activities to just say hello or have a chat. Kaitlyn had the feeling that she'd have more visitors than usual today. Even if they weren't upset, they'd want to compare notes about all that shaking.

Inside the building, Kaitlyn waved to the receptionist. "You make out okay last night?" she asked.

The receptionist shrugged. "My husband slept through it. Glad to have you back."

Kaitlyn laughed and went straight to her office. She put her purse on the desk, took off her jacket, and hung it on the back of the door. Quickly she glanced at her reflection in the mirror. She was blond-haired and blue-eyed, with a freshly scrubbed look that made her appear younger than her twenty-seven years. Visitors to the center often assumed she was a teenaged grand-daughter of one of the residents.

Settling in at her desk, she glanced at the monthly calendar she liked to keep within reach. Today was Tuesday, January thir-teenth. Her friend Abigail's birthday. Kaitlyn was anxious to call her but thought it might be too early. She'd bought her a special present and wanted to take her to dinner. Abigail had a big heart. Her regular visits to Orange Grove to cut the se-niors' hair had come about unexpectedly and turned into one of the events the seniors looked forward to most. Even people who didn't want their hair cut had fun watching the action. It's amazing how some of the best things in life happen by chance, Kaitlyn often thought.

Last June Abigail had stopped by the center after working on a film in the area. She'd accompanied Kaitlyn to the recreation room, intending to stay just a few minutes. Kaitlyn introduced her to the seniors and they started asking questions about the movie. One thing led to another.

"Bet you wouldn't know what to do with my hair," one of the nearly bald men had called out, pulling at the sparse growth on the sides of his head.

"Is that a dare?" Abigail joked.

The whole room had laughed.

"You trust me with a scissors?" Abigail continued.

"Any reason not to?"

"Get up here, then," Abigail had urged. "My kit is in the car. I'll be right back."

Abigail ended up giving ten haircuts that first day and made every single person whose locks she tended feel beautiful or handsome. She promised to come back and she did, every month or two until her accident. Kaitlyn often told Abigail that she understood if Abigail didn't have time for the seniors, but Abigail always insisted her visits to Orange Grove were something she looked forward to.

"Hey, Katie," a familiar voice called from the doorway.

Kaitlyn turned. It was Norman Grass. He suffered from dementia that was only getting worse. But there were certain days when he seemed fine. Today was not one of them. He clearly looked agitated. Maybe he hadn't slept well after the earthquake. Kaitlyn smiled at him. "Norman, how are you this morning?"

"Not good, Katie," he said, stifling a sob. "I just saw on the news that my friend Nicky was murdered!"

"Nicky? You mean?"

"Yes. Nicky Tendril. Remember I told Abigail Feeney he really could use a free haircut? She went to his apartment a few times, then told him she wasn't coming back. I wonder how she'll feel now that he's dead. I bet she'll be happy!"

"Norman," Kaitlyn said, coming around the desk. "Sit down for a minute."

"I don't want to sit down. I just wanted to tell you that your friend was very hurtful to Nicky. He mentioned it every time I talked to him. And now she doesn't come back to see us, either."

Kaitlyn knew what had happened between Nicky and Abigail. She didn't blame Abigail one bit and felt terrible that the whole incident stemmed from Abigail's generosity with the residents of Orange Grove. Abigail worked hard and didn't need to spend her precious time giving free haircuts to someone who was not only rich but rude. "Norman, I told you she had an accident," Kaitlyn said calmly. "She broke her arm. She hasn't been able to work. I'm very sorry about Nicky. What happened to him?"

"Someone threw him against the wall in his apartment. I told him he should have moved in here with us." He turned and stalked down the hallway.

Kaitlyn sighed. Poor Abigail. She's been through so much lately. No wonder she's always saying she's cursed. Kaitlyn went around the desk, picked up the phone, and dialed Abigail's number. I just want to hear her voice and wish her a happy birthday, she thought.

Back in his room, Norman Grass was also picking up the phone. He'd very carefully written down the number of the police hotline that the reporter had repeated three times. He'd give them a piece of his mind regarding that hurtful, greedy Abigail Feeney.

26

Gloria Carson had barely slept. First she couldn't get the sight of Nicky's dead body out of her mind. Then the earthquake struck. Tubes and bottles of makeup that neatly lined the shelves in her little bathroom had gone flying, most of them splashing down into the toilet. Donning rubber gloves, she'd fished the mascara and lipsticks and eye pencils out of the water, tossed them into the trash, and wearily gone back to bed.

All night she kept thinking about the events of the day. One thing that bugged her was the funny way the detectives looked at her. She knew they weren't thrilled that she'd gotten blood around the apartment. But they could have shown an iota of sympathy for my plight, she mused. I was the one who ran to call for help, raced back to Nicky's side, was shocked into hysteria, and what do I get for my troubles? Attitude with a capital *A*.

Sixty-two years old, Gloria had lived in her apartment for five years. She got a break on her rent in exchange for being the on-site manager whom tenants called with their problems. Not that she could fix a leaky pipe, but she made sure it got done quickly. When she first moved in, she tried to be friendly to everyone. Nicky never gave her the time of day. He kept to himself. Gloria worked part-time for a dermatologist to the stars. By the time she got home, Nicky always had his shades pulled down. Their paths didn't cross except when he needed something fixed or she had to remind him to get his wash out of the machine.

Love thy neighbor wasn't something he believed in.

At 7:00 A.M. Gloria got out of bed, showered, and was making do with what makeup she had left when the detectives called and asked if they could come speak to her again. They said they wanted to see if there was anything that they or she missed. It was so unfair. Their pretense didn't fool Gloria one bit. She had watched enough of those crime shows. I live next door. I found the body. It would be so easy for them if I dunnit.

At 8:30, Detectives Vormbrock and Nelson were sitting in her living room. The heavy smell of Gloria's freshly applied perfume was making Nelson's nose itch.

"I hope those television trucks outside don't report that you came in here to question me," Gloria said, dressed and ready for work. She was wearing gold pants, heels, and a white ruffled blouse. Gloria was an attractive woman with teased red hair, who never walked out the door before she'd done herself up. She'd been divorced twice and joked to her friends she was hoping for a trifecta.

"Ms. Carson, we would like for you to tell us what you know about Nicky's routine," Vormbrock began.

"Routine? He was retired and kept to himself. I work during the day and have better things to do than to keep track of his routine."

"So you don't know if he had any regular visitors?"

"No."

"You found his wash in the machine but there was so sign of a maid. Did he clean the apartment himself?"

"I guess so. If he had a maid I never saw her. Or him." She patted her hair.

"Are we making you nervous?" Nelson asked.

"What makes me nervous is knowing I live a stone's throw from where a murderer took Nicky's life. I barely slept a wink last night."

"There was a girl who came to Nicky's apartment a few times and gave him free haircuts. You know anything about that?"

"No, but I wish I did. A good haircut is expensive these days."

The detectives both nodded. Nelson scratched his nose.

Gloria clasped her manicured hands and leaned forward. "Let me tell you something. When I went to work in the morning, I always assumed Nicky was still asleep. As you can see, my front door opens onto Monty Street, his is around the corner on Eastern. I park my car in front of my house. I come home at night and rarely pass his front door. For weeks I wouldn't hear a peep out of him. There are eight apartments in this building. Everyone lives their own life. As long as people pay their rent on time and don't make too much noise, I'm happy. It's just my luck that Nicky turns on a wash right before he's murdered. If I didn't decide that I wanted to throw in a load of towels, he'd still be lying in a pool of blood!"

The detectives were both silent for a moment.

"Ms. Carson," Vormbrock said. "All we want to do is bring Nicholas Tendril's killer to justice. Can you understand that?"

"Of course."

"We're asking you questions in the hope that you'll remember something you hadn't thought of previously. Something that might be helpful for us. That's all."

The detectives stood.

"You have our cards," Nelson said.

"The girls who live in the building weren't any help when you talked to them? I was so upset last night . . . I don't even know when any of them returned home. They all keep crazy hours, running here and running there."

"Every one of them was at work when the murder took place," Nelson told her. "None of them knew of anyone who visited Mr. Tendril."

"Their names aren't on your list of suspects then?" Gloria asked, a touch of sarcasm in her voice.

"Ms. Carson, we're just doing our job."

Gloria was silent as the two men walked out the door. She went back to the bathroom to check her hair and makeup before leaving for work. Is there something I might have noticed yesterday? she wondered. The killer must have left behind some kind of clue.

She started going over in her mind every second from the time she got home yesterday. As usual, she parked her car close to her front door. The sun was so bright. When she'd gotten out of her car she'd dropped her keys, so she leaned down and her sunglasses fell off. After gathering the keys and the sunglasses, she'd gone into her apartment, dropped the mail on a table, and poured herself a cold glass of water. She was home for at least half an hour when she decided to do a wash.

She'd gathered her towels, gone back to the shed, and been annoyed when she discovered Nicky's laundry was in the machine. There was a sign above the washer and dryer that urged tenants to be considerate of their neighbors by removing their clothing as soon as the cycle finished. Unfortunately most people lost track of time. Gloria had hurried to Nicky's back door, half expecting the shade to be pulled down.

So what did I notice? Gloria wondered as she put a few finishing touches on her makeup. I think there was something. I've got to figure out what it was.

If only to save my own skin.

27

Regan had set up her laptop and printer on the kitchen table and was searching the Internet for films currently in production in Los Angeles with Cody's name attached. There were none. There were also no listings for an "Untitled Short Film." If Regan and Abigail tried to go through the thousands of sites about films in production in Los Angeles searching for signs of Cody and Dean's project, it would take forever.

Abigail sat back in her chair. "Regan, they're probably nowhere to be found on any legitimate list. I'm sure they don't have much money and are trying to get people to work for free. Cody said they were planning to meet with investors. Who in their right mind would give those two money to make a film?"

Before Regan could answer, Abigail tapped her forehead with her palm. "People like me, I guess. I can't believe I actually took a pen and wrote out a check to Cody for one hundred thousand dollars."

"You were in love," Regan said. "People do stupid things when they're in love. And it wasn't an investment, it was an IOU. That's different."

"I bet Cody's been turning on the charm with anyone who has a few bucks to throw around. He and Dean probably found people who now believe they're helping to launch the careers of future legends in the industry."

"How much would they need to do a short film?" Regan asked.

"It depends. Some young kids out of film school do it on a shoe-string budget, spending almost nothing. Others manage to get grants. Cody said they wanted their film to have great production values, which obviously costs plenty. You know, Regan, we'd probably have better luck driving around and looking for their camera set up on a street corner than searching the computer."

Regan looked thoughtful. "We could start by going back downtown and showing Cody's picture to the doormen of the high-rises near the bar."

"Will they give out information?"

"They might."

Abigail's cell phone rang. She saw that it was her parents calling. "Here we go with the birthday calls," she said to Regan.

While Abigail told her parents she was fine and that she'd take good care of Grandma, Regan packed up her computer. Abigail had no sooner hung up with her parents when her phone rang again. "I wish I could turn this thing off," Abigail said. "But I guess I can't . . . Hello."

"Abigail, it's Kaitlyn. Happy Birthday!"

"Thanks, Kaitlyn. How are you?"

"I just got back from my trip a couple of days ago. I have a present for you and want to take you out for your birthday one of these nights."

"My grandmother is coming to town today and wants me to invite friends to join us for a birthday dinner this evening. Are you free?"

"I'd love to. Is this the grandmother that—"

"The very one. She's flying out here to buy me a condo but thinks I still have the money she gave me to help pay for it. Lois spotted Cody in downtown Los Angeles two nights ago. My friend Regan Reilly is here from New York to help me track him down."

Kaitlyn's eyes widened. "Wow. And did you hear about Nicky Tendril?"

"Hear about him? The police called to question me. He had a picture of the two of us in his apartment with a line about me being a witch written on it."

"Oh, Abigail, I'm so sorry. This is all my fault!"

"No it's not. But with each passing day, I feel as if I was put on this planet to be paid back for all the rotten things I did in my past life. I'll admit I was stupid to lend Cody money, but the rest of this isn't my fault."

"Of course it isn't," Kaitlyn said as one of the residents of the facility poked her head in the door. "Abigail, I have to go. Where should I meet you tonight?"

"I don't know yet. I'll call you later. Figure we'll have dinner around 7:30."

Abigail hung up. "That was my friend Kaitlyn who works at the assisted living facility that led me to Nicky. She'll join us tonight for the big celebration."

"I'm determined to make it a celebration," Regan said. "We're not going to find Cody sitting here. Let's get in the car and head downtown."

"Okay," Abigail responded as her cell phone rang yet again.

"You're very popular," Regan teased.

Abigail looked at the caller ID. "It says 'Restricted.' " She opened her phone. "Hello?"

"Is this Abigail Feeney?" a man asked, his voice husky.

"Speaking."

"Oh good. I've got a delivery for Princess and Kingsley Martin. I called their house and your number was on the recording. You're their Gal Friday or something?"

"Whatever," Abigail answered. "What are you delivering?"

"Mattresses."

"Mattresses! What for?"

"My guess would be sleeping. How am I supposed to know? My job isn't to ask questions. It's to make the deliveries. If I don't make the delivery, I don't get paid."

"But they'll be back next week. Can't you deliver them then? You'll still get paid."

"I drove here from Arizona. If you don't accept delivery today, the mattresses go back to the warehouse and the Martins get charged extra delivery fees. These are very expensive top-of-the-line mattresses. It says on the order that Princess Martin wants them ASAP."

I don't believe this, Abigail thought. "Where are you?"

"I'm an hour away. It's our company policy to give at least sixty minutes' notice before showing up."

"Okay. I'll meet you there." Abigail hung up the phone and groaned. "I can't take this!"

"What?"

"We have to go to Malibu before we can do anything else today. Princess must have ordered new mattresses. I have to be there to accept delivery."

"Mattresses are being delivered today?"

"Yes."

"But mattresses are usually delivered about five minutes after you buy them," Regan said. "Princess is in Switzerland. When could she have ordered them?"

"Who knows? They're top of the line, of course. Let's get going. We're going to lose so much time."

"You're right, Abigail, we can't lose another minute."

28

Lonnie Windworth woke up with a splitting headache, still wearing his clothes from the night before. He'd been out drinking shots with a bunch of his friends at a bar on Santa Monica Boulevard. It was his buddy's twenty-first birthday, and they were going crazy. Then what happened? Lonnie wondered. He didn't remember leaving the bar. Oh, wait a minute. There was an earthquake. He remembered falling to the ground next to a car.

At least I made it home in one piece, he thought as he sat up in his messy bedroom. Then he saw it. An unfamiliar black bag. A bag whose contents had been dumped all over the floor.

Lonnie owned a black bag he carried to the gym around the corner. But I haven't been there for weeks, he thought guiltily. So I couldn't have mistakenly picked up this one at the gym. It doesn't even look that much like mine. Did one of my friends come home with me and crash on the couch?

Lonnie got up unsteadily and walked through his kitchen to the living room. No one was there. The front door was locked with the chain on it. At least I remembered to protect myself from intruders, he thought.

He went back to his bedroom and sat on the floor where various drafts of a movie called *Untitled* were scattered. Pens, a calculator, a datebook, and various papers and notes were also among the mess.

Whoa, he thought. Whoa. This is not good. I don't remember dumping the bag all over the place at all. He opened the datebook. It belonged to a dude named Dean Puntler who urged anyone who found his datebook to **PLEASE** notify him. He sounds like a nerd, Lonnie thought.

Then he laughed. I must have really been wasted. Not cool. Not cool at all. Lonnie's head was pounding. I've got to take some aspirin, get in the shower, then figure out what, if anything, to do with this bag. I can't bring it to a police station and say I found it. That would be lame. But I feel bad that this dude Dean must be freaking out, wherever he is at this moment.

Lonnie started to stand up but felt sick to his stomach. He lay down on his bed. I'll never do that again, he thought. Never. Why did the bartender keep buying them shots? It was so stupid. How am I going to get to work at the restaurant by 11:00?

He got up again, walked to the shower, and turned it on full blast. Maybe I should just throw the bag in the trash, he thought as he shed his clothes and stepped in the old cracked tub. The water sprayed all over his out-of-shape body. I really should get to the gym he thought as he sat down, leaned his head against the tile, and fell asleep.

29

Abigail's lawyer, Cornelius Cavanaugh, was on the line with Dom Hartman, one of the producers of the movie she'd been working on when she was injured.

"Surely you must be joking," Cornelius huffed. "She broke her arm in two places and you're only upping your offer to twenty thousand dollars?" He laughed. "How will she possibly be able to pay me?"

"That's your problem. She had an operation," Dom said. "She'll be good as new in no time. She doesn't want to get a bad reputation in the business now, does she?"

"How about you?" Cornelius asked. "You're the one with a reputation for accidents happening on your set."

"A few mishaps," Dom insisted. "But they only happen on the set. You know what I mean, Cornelius?"

30

Cody was all ready for the 10:00 A.M. meeting. He looked very L.A., with his expensive blue jeans, crisp white shirt, navy blue designer blazer, and loafers made of buttery leather. He'd dabbed on clean-smelling cologne and perched his trendy sunglasses on top of his head. The effect was dressed up enough to be respectful, yet hip enough to show that he was an "artist."

"You look so handsome," Stella said as she lounged on the couch of their bungalow, picking at a bowl of strawberries.

"And you look absolutely beautiful."

"No I don't. I think I'm getting a zit. It must be the stress of the earthquake."

"Zit or no zit, you'll still be the most gorgeous woman on earth." He leaned over and kissed her. "What are you going to do today?"

"I don't know. I'll figure out something. Maybe I'll sit in the shade by the pool. When will you be back?"

"I'm not sure. But I'll call you. We have a few meetings." He rubbed his hands together. "This time next week, we'll be in Vermont shooting our film! I can't wait. I just saw on the television in the bathroom that they're getting a lot of snow."

"I can't wait either," Stella cooed. "Everything has worked

out so perfectly from the time Dean handed me the script . . .
The fact that my series would be on hiatus at the very time
you're shooting the film so I'd be able to do it . . . The fact that I
met you and fell madly in love . . . The fact that we get to spend
these days together in a bungalow at the Beverly Hills Hotel . . .
It's as if all our stars are in alignment."

Cody's cell phone rang. He glanced at the caller ID. "Dean,
are you outside? . . . Great . . . I'll be right there." He hung up.
"I've got to go." He leaned over and kissed Stella again. "Good-
bye, Beautiful."

Stella laughed. "Good-bye. Hurry back!"

Out in the car, Dean was still in a state of shock after hearing
the news report about Nicky Tendril.

Cody opened the door and bounced in. "Hey, partner," he
said as he pulled the seat belt around him.

"Hello," Dean grunted as he started the car and pulled down
the driveway of the hotel.

"You seem a little tired," Cody said sympathetically. "But the
sleep you lost last night was worth it. Stella was really touched
that you were here. And that rose? That was the best. I'm so
glad I suggested it." He leaned back against the seat, a self-
contented smile on his handsome face.

"Nicky Tendril was murdered," Dean spat as he pulled onto
Sunset Boulevard.

"What?"

"I heard it on the news this morning. Someone shoved him
against the wall. He was found about 3:00 yesterday afternoon.
Not long after we were there eating his rotten soup!"

"Are you kidding?"

"Why would I kid about that? I've got enough troubles."

Cody shook his head and grimaced. "Maybe he tried to serve
that soup to someone else," he joked. "Whew. That guy deliber-

ately waited until after we both politely dispatched those bowls of slop down our throats to tell us that he didn't want to invest in our film. I could have killed him."

"Did you?" Dean asked.

"Did I what?"

"Did you kill him?"

"Are you crazy?" Cody almost shouted. "Of course not. What's wrong with you?"

"Maybe you developed greater impatience after being cooped up in jail for so long," Dean suggested. "After we argued with him, I went out the door first and headed straight for the car. You were a minute behind me. Maybe you shoved him after I left."

"I didn't touch him. How can you think that?"

"Because we were right there before he died and we certainly had the motivation. If you didn't do it, then who did?"

Cody flung up his hands. "I don't know. I wish Abigail had never told me he had all that money. You wasted so much time trying to get friendly with him."

"While you were in jail! You were in jail lifting weights, and I was staking out his house to see if he'd ever emerge and walk up the street to the supermarket. I sat there for days waiting for him to go out for a quart of milk! He finally does and I pretend to bump into him at the store, then offer to carry his groceries home and we start to talk. He was an amazingly boring old man. The whole process was laborious and we don't end up with one dime! Now the cops could find out we were at the scene of the crime right before it happened. Are you sure you didn't give him a little push?"

Cody slammed the seat. "I'm sure! But we didn't leave anything behind, did we? It's better if the cops don't know we were there. For a lot of obvious reasons."

"I didn't leave anything there. I just hope he cleaned our

DNA off those soup spoons before he passed over," Dean sputtered.

Cody pointed at Dean accusingly. "And what about the bag you lost? That's no help to us."

"I didn't lose it! Someone stole it out of my trunk."

"Is there anything in there that could get us into trouble?"

"Like what?"

"I don't know."

"Don't worry, Cody. The postcards you sent me from jail are home in my scrapbook."

Dean pulled through the gates at the entrance to Bel Air. The sun was shining and the perfectly manicured gardens were beautiful. The two drove in silence up the winding roads, passing one mansion after another, until they finally reached the imposing white-columned home of Thomas L. Pristavec.

"Not too shabby," Dean muttered. He identified himself on the intercom at the entrance to the property. The gate clicked open and he pulled down a driveway, which was more like a courtyard, and parked his car next to a brand-new Bentley. "Twenty-five thousand dollars is a drop in the bucket for a guy like this," he said as he reached in the backseat for the leather briefcase he used only for these meetings.

Cody opened his car door, then turned to Dean. "I don't care how much money he has. He'd better not try and serve us any sauerkraut soup."

31

From the moment Lois awakened, she was feeling disappointed that she wasn't free to join Abigail and Regan in their search for Cody. *I only wish I could have thrown a net around him the other night,* she thought.

She showered, dressed, put on a pair of gloves, and hurried outside. Her next-door neighbor Hank, a twenty-year-old surfer, was just coming out of his door in a wet suit and looked half asleep.

"What's happening, Lois?"

"Not much. How are you doing, Hank?"

"The earthquake freaked me out a little," he drawled. "An empty beer bottle fell off the coffee table and smashed. I knew I should have thrown it out a few days ago."

Lois laughed. "The water glass I keep next to my bed broke." She paused. "How will the earthquake affect the surf?"

"I'm going to find out right now. Nice gloves. You have a different pair on every time I see you. They're always so chic."

"You need your wet suit for protection from the elements, I need my gloves. Because I have to wear them every day, I like a little variety."

"Cool. I don't care what my wet suit looks like as long as it keeps me warm."

"Have fun. Hope you catch a big wave," Lois said as she went down the stairs and out to her car. She programmed her cell phone into the car's speakers and called Abigail as she started down the road. When Abigail answered, Lois cried, "Hey, Birthday Girl!"

"Hey, Lois, I spoke to my grandmother. She's taking a few of us to dinner tonight. You have to join us."

"Great. Where?"

"Not sure yet. You do okay with the earthquake?"

"I was fine. No problem."

"That's good. I can't talk now but I'll call you later and let you know where we'll meet. Probably around 7:30. If your shoot runs late, just get there when you can."

"Okay. Before you hang up tell me what happened last night when you went downtown."

"We showed Cody's picture to the bartender and the waiters at Jimbo's but nobody remembered ever seeing him."

"Too bad. Well, good luck today. Let me know if there's any good news to share."

"Don't worry, Lois. You'll be the first to know."

32

Cody and Dean walked up the steps to the enormous front door of Pristavec's mansion. Dean rang the bell.

"I had no idea the house would look like this," Cody whispered.

"Me neither. Last time I met him in a restaurant. I guess he trusts me now."

The door was opened by a butler. "May I help you?"

"Mr. Pristavec is expecting us," Dean said. "My name is . . ."

The butler nodded. "Come in, please."

Something tells me we're not going to be forced to eat lousy sauerkraut soup, Cody thought as they stepped into a magnificent marble entryway.

"Mr. Pristavec will receive you in the living room," the butler informed them. "Follow me."

"Anything you say," Dean said nervously, clearly awestruck and intimidated by the elegant surroundings. A grand staircase at the other end of the long foyer went up to the second floor. Framed portraits hung on the wall next to each step. This is unreal, Dean thought. If Pristavec saw my crummy apartment, he'd never in a million years trust us with his money.

They followed the butler around the corner and down two

plushly carpeted steps into a living room that was unlike anything either of them had seen before. Where do you even find furniture like this? Dean wondered. Where? Everything here is on such a grand scale!

The seventy-year-old dark-haired Thomas Pristavec was standing in front of a floor-to-ceiling stone fireplace, engaged in conversation with a very attractive woman who appeared to be in her mid-forties.

"Sir, your guests have arrived," the butler announced.

Thomas turned his head. "Hello, Dean!" he called enthusiastically as he hurried over and shook his hand. "And, Cody?"

"Yes, Cody Castle, sir."

"Cody, it's so nice to meet you." He turned. "Kicky, come over and say hello."

The brown-haired, brown-eyed Kicky smiled warmly as she walked over and extended her hand to Cody. "It's so nice to meet you."

Cody shook her hand. "My pleasure."

"I love your firm grip," she said.

"Thank you. Your hands are so lovely and soft," Cody flirted back.

Thomas slapped Cody on the back. "They better be! She's a hand model. I think she makes more money than I do. Kicky and I just met a couple weeks ago in Aspen, and I feel like the luckiest man in the world."

Cody hoped that Dean wouldn't faint.

"A hand model?" Dean said as he shook Kicky's hand. "That's so interesting. I'd love to hear all about it."

Kicky waved her beautiful hand. "There's not that much to say."

Wanna bet? Dean thought.

"I've enjoyed the work," Kicky continued. "Only problem is

you always have to be so careful to not get a scratch, or, God forbid, develop a freckle, or—"

"What about a wart?" Thomas interrupted. "That would put you out of business, wouldn't it, honey?" He started to guffaw, clearly amused with himself.

Kicky smiled and rolled her eyes.

"Don't you wear gloves for . . . ? " Cody began. The words were barely out of his mouth when he felt Dean's body tense. He knew what Dean was thinking. Don't say anything that will in any way associate us with, or bring to mind, the annoying Lois. Kicky might very well know her.

"Gloves? Sometimes I wear them, but not in the house. I'm careful." She patted Thomas's arm. "And now I have Thomas to pamper me."

"Yes, you do," Thomas affirmed. "Hey, boys, have a seat. Care for a cup of coffee?"

"No," Dean said quickly as they sat. He wasn't in the mood to take a stab at proper etiquette while being served coffee by a butler, never mind the worry of spilling even a drop on the couch. "We've both had breakfast."

"We have," Cody said. "I'm staying at the Beverly Hills Hotel. The breakfast I ordered from room service was just amazing. Their fruit is so fresh."

"Oh sure," Thomas said. "Sure, sure, sure. Love that place. Especially the Polo Lounge."

"It's a great spot," Dean agreed. "I just love going there, too."

"Glad everyone is well fed. Now let's get down to business," Thomas said. "Cody, it's great to meet you. Kicky and I are excited about the project. We really loved the script. Loved it. As I said, we met in Aspen, so we both really enjoyed the skiing background."

"I've been going to Aspen every Christmas but I hadn't skied for years," Kicky explained. "I was afraid of breaking a hand. But now that I've met Thomas, I'm risking it. Thomas doesn't want to ski without me."

"No, I don't."

"How romantic," Dean said, trying to sound touched. "Of course our story is set in Vermont."

"Oh, that's right," Thomas noted. "Vermont it is. Well, as I said before, I like the idea of investing in a movie that's only thirty minutes long. You promise it's not going to run one min-ute over?" He laughed heartily as did Kicky.

"We promise," Cody said.

"Now, you think you'll be able to sell this to cable?"

Dean cleared his throat. "The possibilities are endless. Cable, foreign rights, DVD sales . . . an Academy Award?"

"Wouldn't that be fun?" Thomas laughed. "Then I'd really have a big party. You promise our star will be there?"

"Oh yes. Stella would be thrilled to come."

"We would have loved to meet her now," Kicky said.

"She's so busy," Dean replied earnestly. "She's got that series in New York—"

"Listen," Thomas interrupted, "I think you guys are great. I really do. Don't you, Kicky?"

"They are lovely young men."

Thomas grabbed her hand and kissed it, then held it up to Cody and Dean. "Can you believe how gorgeous? For most hand models work is over by the time they're Kicky's age."

"Thomas!" Kicky protested.

"I'm proud of you, baby." He turned back to Cody and Dean. "Listen, fellas, I know we were talking about a twenty-five-thousand-dollar piece of the pie."

Uh-oh, Dean thought. Please don't cut us down. We need every penny.

"But what I would like to do is invest more. I believe I'll make money on this. If not, I'll just make sure Kicky never stops working." He laughed. "I know you were closing up the investments, but do you have room in the deal for me to buy two shares? I'd like to invest fifty thousand dollars."

Dean unconsciously licked his lips, like a dog waiting for a treat. Inwardly, Cody cringed. "Sir, we would be able to accept that, yes," Cody said. "One of our investors just passed away unexpectedly. We hadn't received his money and we don't want to bother the family in their time of grief."

"That's a shame," Thomas said. "I would have invited him to my screening."

"I'm sure he would have enjoyed himself," Dean said solemnly.

"Okay then," Thomas said. "I'll have my accountant drop off a check here this afternoon."

"That's fine. We'll swing by later and pick it up," Dean offered.

"I've got a better idea," Thomas said. "You said you love the Polo Lounge so much? Let's meet there tonight. Kicky and I insist on taking you two for a celebratory dinner."

"Oh, no, please," Dean protested, willing his voice not to squeak. "We don't want to put you out. Honestly, that's so generous but—"

"We insist," Thomas said forcefully.

Blood was rushing to Cody's head. "You're being so kind, but honestly—"

"We insist," Pristavec repeated. "If you want that check, meet us at the Polo Lounge tonight. Seven-thirty good for you, Kicky?"

"Perfect. We'll be there at 7:30 on the dot."

33

"Why don't I drive?" Regan had suggested to Abigail when they went down to the car. "You're getting so many phone calls. Even though you can talk on the speaker phone, I think it would make sense."

"Good idea, Regan."

They took Laurel Canyon to Sunset Boulevard and turned right. Traffic was heavy, the way it usually was on a weekday morning. People were out, heading to work, going about their daily life. Despite the previous night's earthquake, it was business as usual in the Southland.

After Abigail spoke to Lois, Regan asked, "Is there anyone else you want to invite to dinner tonight?"

"Not really. If somebody calls to say happy birthday and I feel like inviting them, I will." Her phone rang. She looked at it. "My lawyer." She flipped her phone open. "Hello?"

Cornelius was leaning back in his leather chair, phone in hand, staring out the window of his opulent office. He never tired of his view of the HOLLYWOOD sign. At the sound of Abigail's voice he boomed, "Abigail, how are you? Survive the earthquake in one piece, I trust."

"Right now the earthquake is the least of my problems, Cornelius. And my arm still feels as if it's in pieces."

Cornelius lowered his voice. "Keep your chin up, Abigail."

"I'm trying. What news do you have for me? I can already tell it's not good."

Cornelius whirled his chair around to face his desk and sat upright. "The producers are giving me a hard time," he said with a grim whisper. "They upped their offer to twenty thousand dollars and insist that's as high as they'll go. After all, you already got paid for the whole shoot."

"Of course I was paid for the whole shoot! I was injured on the last day! And I haven't been able to work since!"

"I know. I'm just passing along information. They would be really happy to just settle the whole darn thing."

"So would I! But I'm not accepting that. It's a pittance. I don't even know when my arm will be healed so I can work again."

"I understand. But they insist that's their best offer and won't budge on the amount."

"Then we'll sue."

"That will cost money."

"Doesn't everything?"

"Abigail, you're low on funds. They've hinted to me that this could hurt your career . . ."

"Cornelius, if you don't want to represent me, I'll get another lawyer. They shouldn't get away with their continued carelessness. That scaffolding had already fallen down a couple of times before I was hurt, and they didn't fix it properly. I'm not going to let them bully me. My arm is so sore and—"

"Okay!" Cornelius interrupted, pounding his desk. "I'll call them right now and tell them we don't accept the offer."

"You do that."

"Don't worry about a thing, Abigail. I'll get back to you."

Abigail hung up and looked at Regan. "I didn't invite *him* to dinner."

Regan shook her head and laughed. "I like to see you standing your ground."

"I feel as if I've got nothing left to lose."

When they reached the Pacific Coast Highway, Regan stopped at a traffic light. Across the road, the ocean stretched out in front of them. "I just wish we had some idea of where Dean and Cody's bachelor pad was," she said.

"Malibu stretches for twenty-one miles," Abigail replied. "Most people live close to the highway, but the bachelor pad was supposedly up in the canyons. It was a sublet in the garage of an old house. That's why I didn't make a big deal about seeing it. If Cody had been living on the beach, I would have wanted to visit on weekends no matter what it looked like. We would have spent the days outside anyway."

Regan tapped the steering wheel. "If we only knew of a place where Dean and Cody hung out."

"There's a nude beach we could try."

Regan laughed as she made the right turn onto the highway. "No thanks."

"With my luck, we'd both end up with a sunburn," Abigail said, leaning against the car door and staring out the window. "Believe me, Regan, I've looked for them a million times out here."

Regan drove up the winding narrow highway, the coastline on their left, the canyons on their right.

"Malibu is spread out but the population isn't that large," Regan noted. "Did Princess ever meet Dean or Cody?"

"If she met Dean, she never told me. She met Cody once

when he picked me up at her house. Princess asked us to stay for dinner, but we had plans in town."

"So they didn't get to know each other at all?"

"No. Cody came in the house for a few minutes and made small talk with Princess and Kingsley, but that was it. When we got in the car, he told me he thought they were weird and would never have wanted to stay for dinner whether we had plans or not. Sometimes he was a little opinionated. He asked why I'd want to associate with such wannabes. I reminded him wannabes need haircuts, too, and I was getting paid very nicely." Abigail sighed. "It was honest work, something he didn't know about."

"Does Princess know that Cody split with your money?" Regan asked.

"No. I broke my arm shortly after Cody disappeared, so I didn't come out here again until Princess called and asked if I'd like to look after the house while they were away. She knew I'd had the accident and could use the money. Last week before they left, I drove out here to pick up the keys and go over what I needed to do. It was the first time I'd seen Princess in over three months. They were busy getting ready for the trip so we didn't chitchat. If I had cut her hair after Cody disappeared, I probably would have given her all the dirt. That's what happens when you cut people's hair for a while—you tell each other things you might not even tell your closest friends. As of now, Princess just thinks we broke up. You know, Regan, after a while it gets embarrassing to admit to people how stupid you've been. I'd already told the story to enough people."

"Cody knew that Princess and her husband had money though."

"Of course. Why?"

"If he and Dean needed money for their movie and knew that Princess and her husband were quite wealthy . . ."

Abigail shook her head. "Bad as Cody is, I would find that hard to believe. Besides, wouldn't he have been afraid that I told her he ran off with my money?"

"You're right. But they sound like the kind of people who would just love to invest in a movie like Cody's. My guess is they'd have the chance to be more involved than if they'd invested in a big film. Dean could have done the initial work, testing the grounds to see what Princess and Kingsley knew about your breakup."

"And Princess wouldn't have told me she invested in his film?" Abigail asked, her voice rising.

"I don't know. I'm just trying to explore every angle. If she thinks you and Cody broke up without any hard feelings, she might have convinced herself it's something okay to do."

"I'd consider that a stab in the back," Abigail said vehemently. "There would be no excuse for that. We shared secrets. I'm telling you, there's a code you have with your hairdresser. Or at least there used to be."

"I'm not saying Princess is involved with the film in any way. But Cody is clearly an opportunist. That's all I'm thinking. He's the type who would use your contacts behind your back."

Regan turned off the highway, heading toward the water, then steered the car up the long driveway to Princess and Kingsley's residence. The sight of the house in the daylight, perched on a bluff with the sun sparkling off the waters of the Pacific in the distance, was certainly impressive. "Now I can really appreciate what a wonderful setting this is," Regan said.

"Location, location, location," Abigail answered. "But they still can't sell it."

"Does Princess really need to be that close to Beverly Hills?"

"Yes," Abigail answered flatly.

Regan laughed.

"The woman loves to shop," Abigail continued. "She's bored out here by the beach. She said there are only so many sunsets you can admire."

When they got out of the car, Regan walked to the edge of the property and looked out at the horizon. The air smelled fresh, and a slight wind was blowing. The ocean was crashing against the cliffs far below. She turned and walked toward the front door. "That water is closer than I thought."

Abigail had just retrieved the keys from her purse. "That's another problem. Besides the murder that took place here, which is a turnoff, many people are convinced this house will do a cannonball off the cliff one day." She unlocked the door and pushed it open.

"In that case, I hope the delivery man gets here soon."

Abigail turned off the alarm, did a quick walk through the house, then joined Regan in the living room. As they waited, two of Abigail's childhood friends called to wish her a happy birthday. Regan was deep in thought, going over her notes.

At 10:30, Abigail looked at her watch. "He was due here half an hour ago."

"You don't have his number, do you?

"No."

"Let's wait a while and see what happens," Regan proposed.

Another half an hour passed.

"This is ridiculous," Abigail said impatiently. "We're wasting precious time."

"I thought there was something fishy about that call," Regan said slowly.

"You did?"

"I didn't want to say anything because you've got enough to

think about today, and you couldn't *not* come out here. But I'm surprised Princess wouldn't have warned you that mattresses were going to be delivered. You were supposed to check the house every day but not at any specific times, right?"

"Right. As a matter of fact she preferred that I come at different times so there was no established pattern of the house being empty. She never said anything about waiting for deliveries. I didn't want to bother her while she was on vacation, but I think I will." Abigail got up, walked into the kitchen, picked up the phone, and pushed the speed dial for Princess's cell phone.

Regan was right behind her.

"Hello, this is Princess. Sorry I can't answer your call . . ."

"Her voice mail," Abigail said to Regan then stopped abruptly, her eyes widening. "We're on a plane heading back home. If you need immediate assistance . . ."

Abigail hung up. "Regan, this is so strange. The voice mail says they're on their way home. They weren't due back until Friday."

"How long have they been gone?"

"A week."

"That's enough vacation for a lot of people. All of a sudden they want to sleep . . . in their own bed." Regan raised her eyebrows. "Or are anxious to try out their new mattresses."

Abigail sank into a chair at the kitchen table. Her face crumpled. "Regan, what am I going to do? This all seems so hopeless. We'll never find Cody. He's probably spent all my money anyway." Tears filled her eyes.

"Come on, Abigail," Regan said quickly. "We're going to do everything possible to find him today. We'll give the mattress man another fifteen minutes then we're out of here. If he shows up and we're not here, he'll call you again. We'll come back and give him a good tip for all his trouble."

Abigail took a tissue from her pocket and dabbed her eyes. "That's an idea."

"And a good one, if I do say so myself. Don't cry, Abigail. Have you ever heard the saying 'If you cry on your birthday you'll cry all year'?"

"Yes, Regan, I have," Abigail answered, a welcome twinkle in her eye. "It's one of Grandma Ethel's expressions."

Oh brother, Regan thought, as they both laughed. "Some comfort I am. Abigail, let's lock up and wait outside. Standing in the sunshine for a few minutes will make you feel better. If no one shows up soon, we're out of here."

"We'll head downtown?"

"Yes."

"Okay, Regan," Abigail said, her voice slightly shaky. "Thanks again for being here with me. You're a big comfort. I don't know what I'd do without you . . ."

Abigail's cell phone rang. She had left it on the coffee table in the living room. "Maybe the delivery guy got lost," Abigail said hopefully as she hurried out of the kitchen.

But it wasn't the delivery man.

Detective Vormbrock was calling. He and Detective Nelson wanted to have another chat with Abigail.

34

Nora loved staying at the Breakers Hotel. She and Luke usually went down for ten days every January. By then the holidays were over, she'd have finished her latest book, and they could enjoy some rest and relaxation. This year the weather was even warmer than usual, which put lounging by the pool at the top of Nora's to-do list. And that's exactly what she was doing.

Luke had once again gone to play golf. Later they'd join friends for drinks and dinner. After a light lunch, Nora had staked out one of the lounge chairs in the back row and set up camp. She planned to relax there until it was time for her 3:30 massage appointment in the spa. Wearing a wide-brimmed hat and sunglasses, she applied suntan lotion then pulled a newspaper out of her bag.

The headline announced the earthquake in Los Angeles. Nora sighed. I was sitting here yesterday when Regan called to say she was going to Los Angeles. Who'd have thought I'd be sitting here twenty-four hours later reading this?

Nora devoured every word about the earthquake, then felt her eyes starting to get heavy. This is crazy, she thought. I certainly slept last night. I guess I'm catching up on needed shut-eye. She put down the paper, lowered the beach chair to a more comfortable angle for snoozing, and closed her eyes. The sounds of activity around the pool were in their own way relaxing. No one was chattering loudly but conversations still reached Nora's ears.

Then she heard the scraping of chairs. She opened her eyes for a moment. Two women were sitting down nearby, positioning their chairs to face the sun. They were both very attractive and shared a love of expensive jewelry.

"Judy, I'm so glad I ran into you. I flew down here the minute my divorce papers came through. It's nice to finally spend some of that miser's money without asking permission. He never gave me an extra cent. It was all for his kids, nothing for my son."

"How is your son?"

"He was in Los Angeles last night during the earthquake. When I heard about it this morning, I called his cell phone and told him it would have been nice to let his mother know he was all right."

The other woman laughed. "My son is the same way. He took off for Europe last summer and do you think he called to let us know how he was? No. We'd get one-sentence e-mails. Now he has a girlfriend, so I hope he'll settle down a bit more. Is your son seeing anybody?"

"He mentioned something about an actress. I don't know . . ."

Nora felt like raising her hand and saying, "My kid was there for the earthquake, too!" Feeling groggy, she drifted off to sleep. When she woke up, the two women were gone.

35

By the time Gloria parked her car in the lot of the Beverly Hills office building where she worked, she was even more irked than before. She was trying to remember what she had seen yesterday that struck her as unusual, but all she could think about was those two detectives. They looked as if they'd like nothing better than to send me to the electric chair, she thought.

Well, at least I'll have to focus on other things for the next few hours, she reminded herself as she rode in the elevator from the garage up to the office of Dr. James Cleary, dermatologist to the stars. It will be an escape from all that craziness back at the homestead. How wrong she was.

"Gloria, you're here!" Nicole gasped as Gloria walked through the door. Nicole was one of the stylish twenty-something young women who worked in the office. She and Gloria answered the phones. "Are you all right?"

"I've had better days."

Nicole held up the newspaper. "Tara just saw this. It said you found your neighbor's dead body! Oh my God! We didn't think you'd come to work."

"It was horrible," Gloria said as she hung up her coat. "But I certainly didn't want to stay home with nothing to do but obsess over everything that happened."

Dr. Cleary, a man of few words, was sympathetic. "Gloria, if there's anything I can do for you," he said gravely, patting her arm.

"How about a free round of Botox?"

Cleary pretended to laugh. "I'm glad to see you can joke about it," he murmured, then disappeared down the hall to his private office.

I guess that means no, Gloria thought. She came around the desk, sat in her chair, and was ready to take on the day. But flashes of the scene surrounding the discovery of Nicky's body kept replaying in her head. What was it that gave me pause? she wondered. What struck me as unusual?

The phones started ringing, knocking her out of her reverie.

"I need Botox."

That makes two of us, Gloria thought as she gave the caller an appointment.

Another caller sounded tentative. "I would like to try Restylane on my wrinkles. Does it really help?"

"Restylane works wonders. It restores volume and fullness to your face. Dr. Cleary is a genius," Gloria said as if by rote. "Would you like an appointment?"

"I'm a little nervous. Aren't there people who really overdo it? I was looking through a celebrity magazine and—"

"They didn't come to this office," Gloria interrupted. "Call us when you're ready to have the procedure."

Gloria answered the phone again and heard, "Hello, my name is Stella Gardner."

"How can I help you, Ms. Gardner?"

"I have a pimple that developed overnight. I can tell it's only going to get worse. I need to have it treated as soon as possible. Can I make an appointment for today?"

"I'm sorry, Ms. Gardner, but Dr. Cleary is booked for the next three weeks. I can give you an appointment on February second."

"I can't wait that long! I'm on a television show and have to film again on Friday."

"What show is that?"

"*Crimes Most Passionate.*"

"Just a minute, please." Gloria put Stella on hold and turned to Nicole. "Have you heard of Stella Gardner from *Crimes Most Passionate?*"

"I love that show!" Nicole said excitedly. "Stella Gardner is so fabulous."

Gloria released the hold button on the phone. "Ms. Gardner, we just had a cancellation. What time can you get here?"

"I could make it by noon."

"We'll be at lunch. How about 1:30?"

"Perfect!" Stella replied. "Thank you. I was so upset about the earthquake my skin broke out."

You should know what my night was like, Gloria thought. "Dr. Cleary will take care of your problem," she said. "See you later, Ms. Gardner."

"Yes, you will!" Stella said enthusiastically.

She must think her arrival will make my day, Gloria mused as she hung up the phone. Her mind flashed again to the sight of Nicky's dead body. I just have to remember what it was I saw, she thought, suddenly feeling an overwhelming sense of urgency. When I get home, I'm going to retrace my every step from the moment I got out of my car yesterday. I'm sure I noticed something unusual. I've got to figure out what it was.

Stella Gardner's visit won't make my day, she thought as she fluffed up the ruffles on her blouse. What will really make my day is when I manage to show up those detectives.

I've got to do it.

36

S ee you tonight! Looking forward to it," Dean gushed as he and Cody were saying their good-byes to Pristavec and Kicky in the exquisite foyer that was more than twice the size of Dean's apartment.

"Oh sure," Pristavec bubbled, slapping Dean on the back for the umpteenth time. "It'll be fun. You know, I made a lot of money in a lot of businesses. But I never tried showbiz before. I'm super-excited."

"Never tried showbiz?" Cody said with a smile. "Have you lived in L.A. for very long?"

"No," Thomas said. "I lived in Minnesota most of my life. After I retired, I decided to move someplace warm. Here I am. I'm loving it. Just loving it. It's the best." He slapped Cody on the back. Cody slapped him back.

Dean, feeling compelled, slapped Pristavec. This is like a scene from The Three Stooges, Dean thought.

"Thanks again," Cody said, inching out the door.

"Hey, fellas, why don't you make the dinner reservation?" Pristavec suggested. "If you do it in person, we might get a better table." He winked and rubbed his fingers together. "Grease the palm a little, eh?"

"Sure," Cody answered. "We'll do that."

They escaped out to the car as fast as possible, without seeming rude. Kicky and Thomas watched, and waved at the car as they drove away.

Cody waved back until they were out of sight.

"Cody, why did you have to mention the Beverly Hills Hotel?!" Dean suddenly screamed as they started down the winding road.

"I thought it would sound good."

Dean sighed. "And I can't believe she's a hand model! My God!"

"How many hand models can there be in Los Angeles?" Cody asked. "I'd love to know if she's met Lois."

"I wouldn't. The last thing we need is anything else about you getting back to Abigail before we can hightail it out of town."

"Poor Abigail," Cody said. "Today's her birthday. I feel bad. I do miss her . . ."

"Please refrain from making any birthday calls," Dean grunted.

"You don't have to worry. I was supposed to pay her back today."

"You're joking."

"You knew that, didn't you?"

"No. I knew you'd borrowed money, but I had better things to do than to keep track of when your payment was due."

They were both silent for a moment. "Hey, Dean," Cody said, patting him on the shoulder. "Don't forget! We're getting fifty thousand dollars from that guy!"

Dean shrugged. "That's the first good thing that's happened today. It feels like the first good thing that's happened to me in ages."

Cody furrowed his brow. "How did you meet Pristavec?"

"You're not going to believe it."

"Try me."

"We met on line for popcorn at the movies."

"You're kidding!"

"No. I was by myself. He was by himself. We started chatting about movies and then he got his popcorn and went in to the theatre. On the way out I saw him again and asked what he thought of the film. We both loved it. I gave him my card and told him about our project. Right away he said he'd like to hear about it and asked if we could meet for lunch the next day. That was it! That was right before you got sprung from the Big House. We had lunch, then he was leaving for Aspen where he met the lovely Kicky. Believe me, I had no idea he had that much dough."

"It just goes to show, you never know, do you? You never know what's going to happen today. Or tomorrow, for that matter."

"You should be the poster boy for that sentiment," Dean said. "You're in L.A. one day, in the can in Texas the next."

"Dean, buddy, you're hurting my feelings."

"I don't think that's possible. Anyway, there's a lesson for us here. If you meet someone at a movie theatre, they must like movies, right? Next time we need money for a film, we'll scan the crowd at the Cineplex."

"What are we going to do about Stella tonight? She'd be upset if she thought we were lying about not having all the money in place. She wanted to go someplace great for dinner."

"Not to mention that I implied she was in New York," Dean added. "It's your fault we're going to the Polo Lounge, right in the hotel where she will be."

"What's done is done," Cody said. "We'll have to figure out some kind of plan."

"I'll take the Scarlett O'Hara approach and think about

it later," Dean said, then glanced at his watch. "It's not even 11:00. Our next appointment is at 2:00. What do you want to do? And don't tell me you want to go back to the hotel. I refuse to take you there."

Cody laughed. "Why don't we go to the movies?"

"Not a bad idea. I don't think we'll happen upon any potential investors, but you've got to stay out of sight. There must be a good movie playing in Westwood. Let's head that way."

37

Kaitlyn was busy all morning, which wasn't surprising. She had a lot of phone calls to return after a week's vacation, and many of the residents were stopping by her office. A few of them didn't care at all about the earthquake, they were angry at her for being away.

"Katie, you were gone a long time," a woman named Clara said accusingly. "Why?"

"I went to visit my parents," Kaitlyn said. "I was only gone a little over a week."

"Yesterday was Monday. Shouldn't that have been the day you came back?"

"I had an extra day's vacation so I used it to get things done I don't have much time for," Kaitlyn explained. "I have to go to the doctor sometimes, too."

"Oh," Clara grunted. "Are you healthy?"

"Yes, I am."

"Good. See you at bingo."

At least she seems to have missed me, Kaitlyn thought with a smile. I should feel good about that. And it always pleased her to hear the residents call her Katie. It felt familiar and affectionate. They had taken it upon themselves to address her that way.

Kaitlyn's boss asked her to join him in the conference room at lunchtime. They'd have a bite to eat and catch up. Oscar ran a tight ship but was more than pleased with her performance on the job.

At noon Kaitlyn tapped on the conference-room door.

"Come in," Oscar said. A balding man in his mid-forties, with a thin moustache, he'd worked in the health care industry his whole life. When he saw Kaitlyn, he smiled and stood to greet her. "Hello, stranger. I've got your turkey sandwich, salsa sauce on the side, right here, with a glass of your favorite iced tea."

"Thanks, Oscar," Kaitlyn said as they both sat down at the long table. "What are you having?" she asked, pointing to his plate.

"You know me, nothing spicy. A simple cheese sandwich and I'm happy. Good vacation?"

"Great. But I'm glad to be back. I miss the residents when I'm gone, and, I must say, it warms my heart that they seem to have missed me," she said as she put a napkin on her lap.

"They did miss you. Every one of them loves you."

Kaitlyn smiled and raised her eyebrows. "I had a little problem with Norman today," she said as she reached for her sandwich.

"I know. That's what I want to talk to you about."

"Oh?" Kaitlyn asked, putting the sandwich down on her plate.

"He's very upset. He can't stop talking about his friend who was murdered up in West Hollywood and he can't stop complaining about your friend Abigail."

My friend Abigail? That's an odd way of referring to her when you think of all she's done for the residents here, Kaitlyn mused. Better to just let that slide. "It's such a shame," Kaitlyn said. "Abigail was always so nice to Norman and then agreed to go to Norman's friend's house to cut his hair. Now this."

Oscar paused. "Kaitlyn, Norman called the police."

"What?" Kaitlyn was aghast.

"After Norman saw the report about the murder on television, he called the hotline. A detective got back to me a few hours later. He was asking questions about Abigail and, of course, about Norman. I told him that Norman was a man with problems. Kaitlyn, I certainly hope this doesn't turn into an embarrassing situation for us."

"What do you mean? You don't think Abigail—?"

"I'm not saying I think anything. I just don't want our facility to experience even a whisper of a scandal. Not a hint. As you know the elderly in our care are very vulnerable. It's our job to look out for every aspect of their welfare. Today I'm meeting with a family who want to place their father in a facility like ours because he's been ripped off by everyone from the cleaning lady to phony door-to-door salesmen. If they heard anything about a possible problem with someone who came here to cut hair, they'd never walk through the door."

Kaitlyn shook her head. "Oscar, you know Norman isn't well. Making unreasonable accusations is a symptom of his condition. For anyone to take seriously what he's saying about Abigail is very unfair."

"I understand. But, Kaitlyn, my job is to maintain the wonderful reputation of Orange Grove."

Kaitlyn's eyes flashed. "And what about the reputation of 'my friend Abigail'? Doesn't that mean anything to you?"

"Of course it does. But to be quite frank, the reputation of Orange Grove Assisted Living Facility means more."

38

Every morning Walter got up with the sun, walked to the grocery store on the corner, and bought a large cup of strong hot coffee. Then he'd stroll to the little park near his house, sit on a bench facing the street, and watch the world go by. At that hour of the morning the world consisted mostly of people walking their dogs—big dogs, small dogs, four dogs being walked at once. Walter got a kick out of watching the animals as they caught sight of one another. It was as if they'd been struck by lightning. Some started barking, others whimpered, as they desperately strained their leashes to get closer to their fellow canines.

What Walter really loved was seeing the interaction of dog owners who couldn't be more different. Like the recent brief exchange between a tough guy who was out walking his boxer and an elderly woman on a stroll with her toy poodle. He was wearing a denim vest and a bandana around his head. Tattoos covered his arms, tiny silver chains hung from his nose, mouth, and lips. She was wearing a flowered housecoat and slippers. From half a block away the poodle had yapped relentlessly until the dogs finally met.

"Don't worry," the young man remarked as the dogs sniffed each other. "Brutus is very gentle."

"I can't say the same for Lovey," the woman had trilled. "You'd better move along."

"Whatever you say, ma'am. Have a nice day."

"Lord willing."

Now this is why I get up early, Walter often thought. After he had his coffee, he'd walk around the neighborhood, up one block and down the next, getting his daily exercise before the sun rose high in the sky.

The day after Nicky's death was no different. He'd awakened earlier than usual, but wouldn't leave his apartment until it was light. It's dangerous enough around here, he thought. He lived only three blocks from where Nicky had been murdered.

As soon as the darkness faded, Walter was out the door. He purchased his coffee and went straight to that same park bench, but he didn't enjoy himself at all. He felt so bad about Nicky. He felt bad that Mugs was moving, even though she wouldn't give him the time of day. He knew why but he always held out hope. She couldn't get over her husband. Nicky had been the same way. There was never anyone for him but his wife, and she had died fifty years ago. Walter couldn't imagine that problem. There I was, he thought, married for forty years, and Tulip runs off with the plumber who showed up to fix our clogged-up sink. What a rotten deal.

When Walter finished his coffee, he got up, threw the cup in the trash, and walked toward Nicky's apartment. A news truck was set up outside. Yellow crime scene tape ran across the front door.

I can't believe it, Walter thought. I think I was in shock yesterday, but now reality is setting in. It seems so impersonal to see those people who never knew Nicky standing around in front of his home. All the mornings I walked past here, it was nice just knowing Nicky was right inside. And now he's not. Nicky was certainly crabby, but he didn't deserve to die like that. I wonder when his niece will show up. I wonder when they'll have the reading of the will. That ought to be a dilly.

Walter cut short his walk and went home to make breakfast. At 11:00 he called Mugs.

"Hey, Mugsy, I was thinking. Why don't you come down to the senior center for lunch?"

"Walter, my friend is coming tonight."

"Knowing you, the place is already spic-and-span."

Mugs smiled. "You're right about that."

"Seriously, Mugs, I'm calling in the troops. We have to put our heads together. I truly believe that if we talk it out, we'll come up with something that Nicky once mentioned, or something that we know about him that will help the cops. Because, Mugs, we owe it to Nicky to help find out who did this to him."

"You're right, Walter."

"And we owe it to ourselves to stop them before they strike again."

39

"This can't be happening," Abigail muttered as Regan drove over the mountains on the way back to West Hollywood. "It just can't. I must be having a bad dream."

"Everything will be okay," Regan said, trying to sound confident. "This is what detectives do during an investigation. They question everybody. It's their job."

"But they already talked to me. I told them what I know. This is crazy. I hadn't laid eyes on Nicky since last September. I'm so nervous."

"There's nothing to be nervous about, unless there's something you're not telling me."

"Regan!"

"I'm kidding, Abigail. They're just calling you in to see if you trip up on what you told them before."

"I told them the truth."

"Then that's all you have to do again. What did you tell them about your schedule yesterday?"

"I said I left Brennan's house at around 9:30 in the morning to go check the places I'm house-sitting in Malibu and Burbank. Then I went back to Laurel Canyon and shopped for groceries in the little general store. Then I went back to Brennan's and was there until they called me. That's it, Regan. So you see, I was perfectly free to go out and commit a murder."

"What time did you get back to Brennan's?"

"About 1:00."

"And Nicky was found when?"

"Just before 3:00. He hadn't been dead for long. Which doesn't look good for me. I have no proof that I was anywhere else, no airtight alibi, as they say."

"When did the detectives call you yesterday?"

"Around 6:00. They said they wanted to talk to me because they found my picture. They didn't act like it was any big deal. I told them I'd stop by the police station. It was only when I got there and they started questioning me that I started to feel the situation was a little more serious than they had let on when they called me."

"Abigail, just go in and answer their questions again. That's all you have to do. What makes you appear suspicious is that picture. So what? Nicky was mad at you. Those detectives don't have much to go on at all."

"It's very unnerving to be questioned about a crime that you had nothing to do with, even though certain circumstances make it look like you might have a motive. Like the fact that I had a fight with the deceased, am injured, unemployed, and need money." Abigail sighed. "I suddenly have a greater sympathy for anyone who was ever convicted on the basis of 'circumstantial evidence.' "

"You're not going to be convicted."

"Regan, why don't I drop you off at Brennan's house? Relax for a bit. You must be tired. I'll come back for you if they don't throw me in the slammer. We'll get dressed for dinner and head downtown."

"Abigail . . ."

"I mean it. I don't want you to get mixed up in this. And who knows how long it will take? They might keep me waiting. I'll pick you up as soon as I'm finished."

"I just hate to see you going in there alone."

"I did last night. Besides, who would I introduce you as? The private investigator I hired to help hunt down my ex-boyfriend who owes me money?" Abigail almost laughed. "No, Regan, I don't think that would strengthen my defense. They'll think we're Thelma and Louise."

Regan sighed. "Abigail, are you sure?"

"Yes."

"You don't want to call your lawyer?"

"No! Regan, I'm innocent. Besides, he'll charge me a fortune."

"I just wanted to ask. Okay, then," Regan agreed. "You drop me off. They wouldn't even let me in the room when you're questioned anyway. I'll tell you what I'll do. I'm going to look up the coverage of Nicky's murder online. I'd like to see what's been reported. We haven't seen a newspaper today or watched any television reports."

"I hope they spell my name right," Abigail said as she took the key to Brennan's back door off her ring.

They rode up Laurel Canyon, turned right, and wound their way up to Brennan's house. Regan pulled up to the wooded gate and stopped. "I'll get out here. You don't have to pull into the driveway. Just open that gate for me and then you can back out."

"Okay," Abigail said as she opened the passenger door.

Regan gathered her computer bag and purse from the backseat.

"I hope the next time you see me I'm not wearing stripes," Abigail joked halfheartedly as she pressed in the security code and handed Regan the key.

"You won't be wearing stripes, Abigail, it's not your look. Now good luck. I'm sure you'll be back soon. Then we'll go straight downtown."

"What a day."

The gate swung open. Regan hurried across the driveway and up the back path as the gate swung closed. It's really another world back here, she thought. Everything is so still and silent. She crossed the deck and unlocked the back door.

Inside the house all was calm and deathly quiet. At this time of day the lack of direct sunlight made the woodsy interior seem restful and relaxing. What a good place to bring in a masseuse, Regan thought—set up the table in the middle of the living room; no need to turn down the lights.

Regan closed the door, locked it, and put her computer bag and purse down on the kitchen table. I am tired, she realized. I'd love to just stretch out on the bed for a couple of minutes. But no. I'll look online first.

A creaking sound made her freeze in place. What was that? Then a soft fluttering. Regan turned and looked around. A bird had landed on the sill outside the window above the kitchen sink. Oh, she thought. Okay. I've gotten too used to living in New York City, where it's never this quiet. Suddenly she longed to hear Jack's voice. She pulled her cell phone out of her pocket and called his number. His voice mail picked up. He's probably in a meeting, she thought as she left him a message. I miss him, but why do I feel such a need to talk to him right now? she wondered.

A second bird landed at the window. Regan smiled, then turned and faced the kitchen table. Alrighty, she thought as she unzipped her computer case. Let's see what's been reported about the murder of Nicholas Tendril.

40

In a charming little village in the South of France, Brennan was having dinner with the cast and crew of his latest movie when his cell phone rang. His lawyer was calling.

"Brennan, sorry to disturb you but I know you wanted me to keep you informed."

"About what?" Brennan asked, covering his left ear in an attempt to block the sound of all the conversations going on around him.

"The woman who calls herself 'your wife' is out of jail."

"Oh no."

"Oh yes. Her attorneys are required to let us know when she was released. I just got word. She was sprung yesterday. She only served six months for her last burglary."

Brennan got up from the table and walked to a corner of the small restaurant. "That woman is dangerous, I'm telling you. She's going to flip out one of these days and really hurt someone. When she showed up on the set last year in New Mexico, I was freaked out."

"Do you have an alarm at your house?"

"No . . . I have the security gate."

"You should get yourself an alarm."

"As far as I know, she's never been to my house. It was all those letters she sent to my agent . . . and the e-mails . . . and showing up at the set. She had a fit when they wouldn't let her in."

"At least you're shooting in France now."

"Yes, but I have a house sitter staying at my place."

"You'd better warn him."

"Her."

"It's a woman?"

"Yes. She was the hairdresser on my last film."

"If I were you, I'd call her right now. You should talk to her about having an alarm installed for you immediately. Your 'wife' is so jealous she might see the house sitter as her competition."

"Thanks. I'll call her right now." Brennan hung up and pressed the speed dial for Abigail's cell phone, but it went straight to voice mail. He left a message.

"Hey, Brennan, come on. Dinner's ready," the director called to him.

"Okay!" Brennan had considered calling his house then shrugged off the thought. If Abigail were free to talk to him, she'd pick up her cell phone. She must be out. If I don't hear back from her, I'll try again later.

Brennan hurried back to the table where the owner of the restaurant and his wife were lovingly serving their specially prepared dishes. The thought that he should call the house immediately kept nagging at Brennan. But the food kept coming and he was crowded in at the table. The restaurant owner was saying that they'd been cooking all day for them. It would be rude to get up from the table again. It'll be all right, Brennan thought. I'll call Abigail again as soon as I finish dinner.

41

W hen Abigail walked into the police station, she decided she had had enough of feeling guilty. Regan is right, she thought. I've got nothing to be afraid of. I need to be confident. When she joined detectives Vormbrock and Nelson in a private room, she was sure that the mirror on the wall was one of those two-way numbers she'd seen on television. What suspect hadn't figured that out by now? she wondered. You have to watch only one or two cop shows before you realize that the mirror isn't meant for primping.

"Abigail, we just wanted to ask you a few more questions," Detective Vormbrock said, folding his hands in front of him.

His friendly act doesn't fool me, Abigail thought.

"Abigail, would you say there were a lot of hard feelings between you and Nicky Tendril?"

"On my part none. As soon as I realized . . ."

The detectives waited. "Realized what?" Nelson asked.

Abigail hesitated, then decided to tell them the one thing she'd held back about the day before. "I stopped cutting Nicky's hair when I realized how much money he had. The last time I was there I saw the statement from his brokerage account that he'd left out on the kitchen counter. He had over a million dollars in cash. Imagine my shock. I was cutting his hair for free because I thought his funds were limited. I told him that I was really busy and needed to work more because I had so many bills and probably wouldn't have time to come back again. I was giving him the chance to offer to pay me, which he didn't take."

"You didn't tell us that yesterday."

"I was embarrassed. I thought it would sound bad to say I sneaked a look at one of his personal documents, but it was sitting right there. Let me remind you, this all started because I was donating my time to give haircuts to the elderly residents at the Orange Grove Assisted Living Facility. You can call them. One of the men asked if I'd go to his friend Nicky's apartment and cut his hair." Abigail's eyes flashed. "This is what I get for trying to be a decent human being."

Vormbrock and Nelson were silent for a moment. "Did you tell anyone that Nicky Tendril was a man who had a lot of money in the bank?"

"Yes. I told my friends and I told my family. It's the kind of story you tell people you're close to."

"Do you have a boyfriend?

"No. But I did when it happened."

"So he knew about Tendril's money?"

"Yes."

"Where is he now?"

"Good question. He disappeared on me. Right after I lent him one hundred thousand dollars."

Abigail's words hung in the air.

"You've had your share of troubles lately."

"You think? And today's my birthday. I was born on Friday the thirteenth. It's been like this since the day I was born."

Nelson nodded. "What does your ex-boyfriend do for a living?"

"He and his writing partner are trying to get a movie made.

They wrote a script and were planning to co-direct it. I don't even know what it's called."

"So he'd be someone looking for money," Vormbrock said.

"He already *was* looking, last time I saw him. And I was stupid enough to hand it right over."

"Could we have his name, please?"

"Cody Castle. His partner is Dean. I don't know his last name."

"And you have no idea where Castle is now?"

"No. But a friend of mine spotted him in downtown L.A. on Sunday night."

"Thank you for coming in, Ms. Feeney," Vormbrock said. "We'll call you again if we need you. Are you planning to leave town?"

"No, I'm not. And do me a favor. If you track down Cody Castle, please let me know. I want my money back."

Abigail exited the police station, turned on her cell phone, and listened to the message from Brennan. Oh my God, she thought. A stalker? This morning when I was sitting outside I had the feeling that something wasn't right . . . Is it possible? Abigail quickly dialed Regan's cell phone. There was no answer.

42

Regan found a brief story online about Nicky Tendril's murder. It didn't shed any new light on the subject. Regan then checked her e-mail and scanned the other news of the day. I hope Abigail gets back soon, she thought. We have to pick up her grandmother at 5:00 and it's already 12:30. I really want to get downtown and start asking around about Cody. Because once Grandma gets here, all bets are off. Abigail might be able to stall her for a couple more days but then, if we haven't located Cody, she'll have to admit the money is gone.

What happened to the mattress delivery man? Regan wondered. He still hadn't called back by the time Abigail dropped me off. The whole thing is bizarre.

Regan yawned and stretched out her arms. I think I'll try to nap for a few minutes until Abigail gets back. Regan got up from the table and went down the hall to her bedroom. When she reached the doorway, she gasped.

A wild-eyed, robust young woman with long hair and tattered jeans was sitting on her bed, brandishing a butcher knife. She jumped up and lunged at Regan. She must have been six feet tall.

In a flash, Regan grabbed the doorknob and pulled the

door shut. She could hear the knife graze the wood as the door closed.

"What are you doing in my house?" the woman screamed. "This is my house. I'm going to kill you!"

Regan held tight onto the doorknob as the lunatic on the other side struggled to get the door open. The door banged back and forth, but Regan put her foot up against the wall and pulled back on the doorknob with all her strength. What am I going to do? I could try and make a run for it but the gate is locked. I wouldn't know how else to get off the property.

Regan's cell phone started to ring while the woman raged inside the room. Could that be Jack returning my call? she wondered. Oh, Jack. A few seconds later the house phone began to ring. The machine picked up. She could hear Abigail's frantic voice. "Regan, are you there? Please pick up! Please!"

The crazy woman was stabbing at the door with the knife, screaming. The door was thick so the knife hadn't come through yet. Thank you, Brennan, Regan thought. But it was exhausting to hold the door closed. I don't know how much longer I can do this. The woman was as strong as an ox.

Abigail, come home now, Regan whispered. Please. Hurry.

43

Oh my God, Abigail kept thinking. Oh my God. She dialed Regan's cell phone then the house phone. Cell phone then the house phone. No answer. Why didn't that idiot Brennan tell me he had a stalker? Why? Maybe Regan decided to take another shower. Could she have fallen into a dead sleep?

Abigail didn't believe it for a minute.

Something happened.

Abigail ran back into the station house. Nelson and Vormbrock were standing by a desk talking. Abigail ran over to them. She could barely speak.

"You know I'm house-sitting . . . The actor who owns the house just called. He has a stalker who just got out of jail. My friend's at the house. She's not answering the phone. Please help me! There's so much traffic. It might take too long for me to get there . . ."

"Maybe your friend went out," Nelson suggested.

Abigail shook her head. "No. She doesn't have a car. The house is way up on a hill. She wouldn't have gone for a walk. Please help me!" she screamed.

"Is there a patrol car outside?" Nelson barked.

"Yes, sir."

"Let's go!"

"Thank you!" Abigail cried as she followed them out the door. They all jumped in the police vehicle. Nelson got in the front with a patrolman, Abigail and Vormbrock sat in the back.

"We're going to Laurel Canyon," Nelson ordered.

The patrolman turned on the siren and flashing lights as he tore out of the parking lot.

Abigail was beside herself. "Why didn't he tell me had a stalker? Why? I said I'd watch his house. He offered it to me. I would never have left my friend there alone . . . never . . . never . . ."

"Take it easy," Vormbrock said kindly. "Hopefully this is nothing but a wild-goose chase."

Abigail kept calling both phones. No answer. "I know something's wrong," she cried.

They turned up Brennan's block and stopped at the gate where Abigail gave the officer the code.

"Come on!" Abigail urged as the gate slowly swung open. The police car zoomed into the driveway. They all jumped out of the car.

"Go up the back way!" Abigail yelled.

They ran up the back path and across the deck. The door was locked. Abigail started banging on it.

"Abigail!" Regan shrieked. "Hurry!"

"She's there!"

Vormbrock and the patrolman kicked in the door.

Down the hall, Regan's arms were giving out.

Vormbrock was the first one to reach her.

"She's got a knife!" Regan warned.

Vormbrock put his hand over Regan's on the doorknob. "I've got it."

Regan let go of the door. Her arms felt as though they were about to fall out of their sockets. She moved out of Vormbrock's way.

"Regan!" Abigail sobbed, putting her arm around her friend's shoulders.

"Police!" Vormbrock yelled. "Drop the knife and slide the blade under the door."

"Get out of my house!"

"Now!" Vormbrock ordered.

"This is my house!"

"Drop the knife right now!"

"When will Brennan be home?"

Vormbrock rolled his eyes. "He'll be home later. Now drop the knife!"

The woman howled. The blade started to appear under the door.

Vormbrock, his gun drawn, forcefully pushed the door open. He and the patrolman charged the room, quickly handcuffing the maniacal woman.

Regan and Abigail watched as the disheveled intruder was escorted out, still screaming for Brennan.

"Regan, are you okay?" Abigail asked breathlessly.

"I knew I wanted my arms to get exercise but this is ridiculous." They walked to the living room and sat down.

"Let me get you some water," Abigail offered. She hurried to the kitchen, brought back a tall glass, and handed it to Regan. "I'm so sorry, Regan," she said, wiping her eyes. "I'm so sorry . . ."

"Abigail, what did I tell you about not crying on your birthday?"

"I know, Regan." Abigail chuckled through her tears. "But you could have gotten killed."

"I'm glad it was me here alone and not you. That arm of yours wouldn't have been much help to you. Hey, has the mattress man called?"

"What do you think?"

"I think not."

Detectives Vormbrock and Nelson came into the living room.

"Would you like to go to the hospital?" Nelson asked Regan.

Regan shook her head. "No. I'll be fine. Besides, Abigail and I have a busy afternoon ahead." She turned to Abigail. "Your grandmother is going to be here before you know it. And you know what that means. We'd better get going soon."

"I left my car at the police station."

"Whenever you're ready," Vormbrock said, "we'll give you a ride back."

44

Stella Gardner came through the door of Dr. Cleary's office promptly at 1:30, casually dressed but looking glamorous. She checked in at the desk with Tara.

"Do we have a local address for you?" Tara asked.

"I'm staying at the Beverly Hills Hotel."

"Oh, okay. Could you please fill out this information sheet?"

"Certainly." Stella took the clipboard and sat down in the waiting area.

She really is a beautiful girl, Gloria thought. It doesn't look like there's any pimple on her face though. She's wasting her money. With what Dr. Cleary charges, that girl could buy a truckload of calamine lotion, the old-fashioned remedy for clearing up pimples.

The phones were quiet. Nicole called out to Stella, "I just love your show. You're a wonderful actress."

"Thank you so much."

"Is there anything else we'll be able to see you in?"

"Yes. As a matter of fact, I'll be in a short film that's shooting next week in Vermont."

"I can't wait!" Nicole enthused. "What's the film called?"

"It doesn't have a title yet. But the script is awesome."

"Okay, I'll be looking for it."

Gloria was half listening. Her mind kept returning to the murder. She wouldn't be leaving work until 5:00. Why can't today be one of the days I leave early? she thought anxiously, desperate to get home. She had the feeling that she was going to find the clue that would lead to Nicky's murderer.

45

Walter had managed to get twenty-two people to come to the senior center to talk about Nicky. He was quite proud of himself.

"Quiet, please! Quiet," he said, addressing the group. "Thank you for coming here on short notice. I've called you together because of our friend Nicky Tendril." He paused. "There's a murderer out there somewhere," he said, dramatically pointing out the window. "A murderer who took our Nicky from us. It's our duty to help the police find who that person is."

"Person or persons," Hilda called out. "More often than not there are two people who work together."

Inwardly, Mugs groaned. That one thinks she's Sherlock Holmes.

"We want to catch whoever is involved, whether there were two killers or twenty," Walter said vehemently. "Now do any of you folks remember Nicky mentioning anything that he was worried about? Anything at all?"

They all shook their heads.

"You know the way Nicky was," one of the men answered. "He was very private and mostly kept to himself."

"I think he started to change after that last heart attack," Estelle Hart opined. "It seemed to me he was getting a little friendlier."

"I didn't notice," another man grumbled.

"Whether he was the friendliest guy in the world or not, he didn't deserve to die like that. He was a good soul, and we have to find out why someone wanted to kill him. I suppose the cops will figure it out if money was stolen. They're not saying much yet. Nicky had a lot more money saved than one would have guessed," Walter informed them.

"What was he waiting to spend it on?" Hilda asked.

"Good question. He didn't even have a cleaning lady," Walter answered.

"Yes, he did," Estelle insisted.

"How do you know?"

"When he won at bingo a few weeks back, he joked to me that now he can afford his cleaning lady. I said she must be pretty cheap because he had only won a few dollars. He laughed and said she only came around a few times a month."

"That's a surprise to me," Walter said, scratching his chin. "Every time I went over to watch a game with Nicky, he told me he was exhausted from cleaning the apartment."

"Well, I'll tell you one thing he spent money on," Estelle announced. "The memory of his wife. He missed her so much. That's why he was so crabby. He never got over her early demise. Just last week Nicky mentioned to me that he brought a dozen roses to her grave every Sunday."

"I never knew that," Walter said sadly.

"She's buried in Pearly Gates Cemetery over in the Valley. He visited Tootsie every Sunday, rain or shine," Estelle reported.

"Tootsie?" one of the women asked disdainfully. "Where did she get a name like that?"

"It was Nicky's pet name for her. If she hadn't died, he would have been a much nicer and happier guy. He told me they always had a lot of fun together."

"What was Tootsie's real name?"

"Abigail."

46

Lonnie had a splitting headache. Trying to take orders and serve food was a nightmare. He would have called in sick, but he knew that wouldn't go over well with his boss. Particularly since he hadn't woken up from his shower until twenty minutes before he was due at the restaurant. It would have been impossible to find a replacement on such short notice.

Every time Lonnie had to go into the kitchen, he thought he would pass out. The smells of all the different dishes nauseated him, and the heat was stifling. All he wanted to do was go to bed and drink ginger ale.

I'm paying for my sins, he told himself. And for the additional sin of having stolen that black bag from God knows where. He was really feeling guilty about that. It didn't help that the people dining at his tables were chitchatting excitedly about this film or that script. Everybody in L.A. seemed to have some project going. It made him wonder about poor Dean what's-his-name, the nerd who pleaded for the return of his date book. How was he coping with the loss of all his papers?

I've got to get that bag back to him, if only for the state of my karma in this universe, Lonnie thought. I don't want to end up cursed. I finish here at five. Maybe when it gets dark, I can drop the bag near the police station.

Hopefully no one will see me.

47

The movie Dean and Cody saw was two and a half hours long and it stunk. At times they whispered to each other about whether they should walk out. Ultimately they decided to stay until the bitter end, if only to see how the story was resolved. By the time they left the theatre, it truly felt like the bitter end. The story was never resolved. Both of them were anxious, depressed, and irritated. The movie had hardly been an escape from all the problems they were facing.

Cody was worried about leaving Stella alone for so long, and Dean couldn't stop thinking about his missing black bag. There were so many papers in there he could never replace.

"The problem with that movie is that it had a lousy script," Dean said as he started the car. "Our script is great."

"Your bag with our script is still missing, huh?" Cody asked as he checked his messages.

"Of course it's still missing. Don't you think I would have told you if it had been found?"

"I suppose. Oh boy. Stella doesn't sound happy . . ."

"If she'd come to that movie with us, she'd be really unhappy. I heard they spent eighty million dollars making that piece of garbage! I wish I knew where they got the money so we could send them our script. We're not asking for that much. They should be throwing money at us!"

Cody was still listening to his messages. "Stella said she hopes I've picked out a good place for dinner tonight."

"Tell her you want to dine late. It's very European."

"Where are we going now?" Cody asked.

"We have a meeting with Wendy on Wilshire."

"Who?"

"Our last investor of the day. She lives in one of the condos on the Wilshire Corridor, hence the nickname. I didn't make it up, she did."

Cody was clearly distracted. "I'd better call Stella back." He dialed Stella's cell phone. "Hey, baby . . . We've been running around . . . I know, but we've been so busy . . . You're at the doctor's? . . . Maybe you'd better rest tonight . . . Oh, okay . . . I just thought if you weren't quite up to going out after the earthquake and . . . I promise I'll be back by four, at the latest." He hung up and sighed.

"Stella went to the doctor?" Dean asked, suddenly alarmed. "What's wrong?"

"She has a boo-boo on her chin."

Dean rolled his eyes.

Wendy on Wilshire was excited to see them, and, of course, to meet Cody. She was about forty, blond, very attractive, and wearing a tiger-print skirt that matched the fabric of her couch. They managed to get her twenty-five thousand without too much ado, then politely refused her offer to come back for dinner.

"We'll have dinner as soon as we get back from Vermont," Dean promised as they stood at her door, about to make their escape. "We're just so busy right now. I don't know when we'll have time to eat. We have to go home and work, make phone calls . . ."

"I'm thinking of going skiing in Vermont next week," Wendy purred, tapping her long tiger-print nails on the front door. "Maybe I'll come by the set."

"Of course. We'll be there starting next Monday. Just let us know," Dean said quickly.

When they were back in the car, Dean threw his briefcase in the back seat. "We're going to have more visitors on the set than cast and crew combined. Don't our investors realize we're artists who want to be left alone to do our work?"

"Guess not," Cody said.

"I'm so exhausted, I wish I could just go home and sleep. Why do we have to have this dinner tonight? Why couldn't Pristavec just give us the check?"

"Come to the bungalow," Cody said. "Take a nap on the couch."

"And disturb the two lovebirds?" Dean asked sarcastically. "I don't think so. Besides, I don't want to be there when you break the news to Stella that you're not having dinner with her. I've had enough aggravation."

"Dean," Cody said, putting his head in his hands, "what am I going to tell her?"

"That's your problem. My problem is figuring out where I can get some rest. It doesn't make sense to drive all the way back out to Malibu. There's so much traffic. I'll probably nap in the car."

When Dean finally pulled up the driveway of the Beverly Hills Hotel, Cody turned to him. "Dean, don't be ridiculous. Come inside."

"No. I need time to myself to just chill out."

"Please," Cody coaxed. "I think it'll be easier if we both explain to Stella that we have another meeting."

"I'm sorry, Cody. I want to be alone. I'll park the car somewhere and take a nap. Call me if you need me. Otherwise I'll meet you at the Polo Lounge at 7:30. Go make the reservation."

Cody got out of the car.

A valet greeted him. "Glad to have you back."

Dean drove back to West Hollywood and found a parking spot on the street where he'd lost his bag. He shut off the car, leaned back, and closed his eyes. He was in a deep dark sleep when Lonnie walked by his car on the way home from work, trying to figure out how to get rid of Dean what's-his-name's black bag.

48

Regan, I can't believe that after what happened you still want to go downtown," Abigail said as they got into her car at the police station. Abigail was now the driver. Regan's arms were aching and she didn't trust herself to hold on to anything, never mind the steering wheel of a car.

"I don't want to sit around," Regan said. "We have to find Cody. That's why I came to Los Angeles."

"Regan, I think your trip has already been worthwhile. You saved my life! If I had been alone at Brennan's house when that wild beast made her presence known, I'd probably be dead."

"Anything for a friend," Regan said, gently kneading the muscles in her arms.

"Just wait till I have a word with Brennan," Abigail said, shaking her fist.

"Well, let's wait and hear his side of the story."

"His story is that he hasn't called me back."

"He will. It's late in France now. Maybe he fell asleep. But, Abigail, there's one good thing that came out of this. You and those detectives are on much better terms."

"At least they got to see the terrible things that happen to me, through no fault of my own. Did I ask to house-sit the home of an actor who has a stalker? No."

"I get the distinct feeling that Nelson and Vormbrock want to find Cody as much as we do."

"That's impossible," Abigail said. "Cody should thank his lucky stars if they find him first. Because when I see him, I'll want to tear him limb from limb."

"I think I have an idea of what that might feel like," Regan commented, still massaging her arms. "Abigail, do you think Cody is capable of murder?"

Abigail frowned. "Regan, I don't know what to think. I told him Nicky was wealthy. But I also told him how cheap he was. Cody would have been pretty stupid to have gone after him for money. But that certainly doesn't make him a murderer . . ."

In downtown Los Angeles they stopped at several high-rise buildings near the bar. Regan made the inquiries. None of the doormen recognized Cody.

"I know there's one more apartment building down the block," Regan said. "Let's give it a whirl."

Abigail pulled up and parked at the curb. "I've given up hope," she said.

Regan patted her arm. "It only takes one." She got out and walked to the entrance. A smiling, uniformed young man started to push the revolving door for her.

He looks like he's about twelve, Regan thought. "Thank you," she said pleasantly. "But I'd just like to ask you a question, if you don't mind."

"Certainly."

Regan showed the doorman Cody's picture. "Have you seen this guy anywhere?"

"No, I haven't," he responded too quickly.

Regan knew he was lying. He was so young and didn't have

his poker face down yet. She made sure he saw the twenty-dollar bill she was holding behind Cody's picture.

"But let me think . . ." he said, scrunching up his face.

Regan slipped the twenty into his hand, then produced another out of her pocket.

"Okay, but please. I could get in trouble."

"I understand," Regan said softly. "But this is very important."

The doorman looked around. "He doesn't live here, but he was staying in one of the tenant's apartments for the last couple of days."

"Did he leave?"

"I don't know whether he's gone for good. Last night I was working a double shift. At about eleven o'clock he brought a gorgeous blonde home with him. She looked like she might be an actress. But they left a couple of hours after the earthquake. She was freaked out."

Abigail is going to kill herself, Regan thought. "Where did they go?"

"I have no idea. They came down, and I called them a cab. They had their suitcases with them."

Regan started to reach inside her purse.

"Don't waste your money. That's all I know. And believe me, I could use the cash."

"Thank you," Regan said gratefully. "You've been a big help." She returned to the car. Abigail looked at her expectantly.

"Why don't I buy you a birthday drink before we go to the airport?" Regan asked.

"Regan, tell me. How bad is it?"

"He was there for a couple of days. He brought in a blonde last night. They left after the earthquake because she was scared."

Abigail pounded the steering wheel with her good hand.

"You cry on your birthday . . ." Regan began.

"That jerk!"

"Come on," Regan said. "One glass of wine. Then you face Grandma."

Abigail put the car into drive. "That's it. It's over now, Regan."

"No it's not, Abigail. We'll resume our search after dinner. It ain't over till it's over."

"You know something, Regan? I have the feeling you're going to get along very well with my grandmother."

"Why?"

"That's another one of her expressions."

49

Ethel Feeney's flight had taken off from Chicago's O'Hare Airport, but not before she'd tried to change her seat assignment. First she'd asked the gate agent for an upgrade, but was told the flight was full. Then she'd asked for an aisle seat but was informed that there were no aisle or window seats left.

"But I'm an old lady," Ethel had said, her expression fierce.

"I'm sorry, ma'am. There's nothing I can do. Maybe when you get on the plane, you'll find someone willing to switch seats."

"Who in their right mind would switch to a middle seat? You're cramped and don't even have one armrest to yourself."

The agent had shrugged, then picked up a microphone to make the boarding announcement.

They were now two hours into the flight. Ethel had on the fancy headphones her grandson had lent her for the trip. She was listening to an opera with her eyes closed, happy as a clam in her aisle seat. In the first hour of the flight she'd driven the burly young man next to her crazy, getting up to go to the bathroom three times. Finally he'd thrown in the towel and offered to switch seats. She'd gratefully accepted and hadn't gotten out of her chair since.

Every minute or two, Grandma Feeney's seatmate glared at

her. I know her type, he thought—pretends to be so helpless. I fall for it, and now I'm crammed in like a sardine. He stuffed his newspaper into the seat pocket in front of him, folded his arms, and closed his eyes.

Ethel was thinking about all the fun she'd have with Mugs and Abigail. When she got bored listening to music, she took a calculator out of her purse, along with the list of imperfections to look out for in Mugs's apartment, with dollar amounts written next to each entry. Anything that would bring the price down.

Just you wait, Abigail, honey, Ethel thought excitedly. Together we're going to make every penny count.

50

Detectives Vormbrock and Nelson had been surprised by the turn of events with Abigail Feeney.

"That girl does have some very bad luck," Vormbrock declared as they sat at their desks. "There's no way she had anything to do with that stalker."

"She's lucky she's not dead. We're lucky the stalker is off the streets and that Regan Reilly knew how to protect herself."

"She is a private investigator," Vormbrock said.

"And seems like a good one. She certainly kept calm and in control. Maybe she'll find the ex-boyfriend for us."

An officer came to the door. "I've got a preliminary report from the lab," he said as he walked over and handed it to Nelson, who started to read.

"What have we got?" Vormbrock asked.

"Hairs that matched the victim's, hair from at least three other people . . . and twelve- to fifteen-inch strands of red hair from a synthetic wig." Nelson looked at Vormbrock. "I don't think this guy was into wigs, do you?"

"Don't think so."

The phone on Nelson's desk rang, and he quickly answered it. "Detective Nelson."

"Hello, Detective Nelson, this is Walter Young from the senior citizens center. You questioned us yesterday about Nicky Tendril."

"Yes, Walter. What can I do for you?"

"I got a bunch of folks together today to talk about Nicky and see if we could come up with any clues for you."

"That's very thoughtful. We're very grateful for any assistance from the public."

"There were a couple things I thought you might be interested in."

"Such as?"

"There seems to be some disagreement as to whether he had a cleaning lady or not."

"Okay."

"And the other interesting thing someone brought up is that Nicky cared deeply about keeping his wife's memory alive. Apparently it's what he cared about most. One of the women here said that he brought fresh flowers to her grave every Sunday. I never knew that, and I was the one who spent the most time with him. Truth be told, I feel a little hurt that he didn't share that with me."

"He visited his wife's grave every Sunday?"

"Rain or shine," Walter answered.

"She died a long time ago."

"She did. At least fifty years."

"Where is she buried?"

"At the big cemetery in the Valley—Pearly Gates."

"Thank you, Walter. Keep us posted. We do appreciate your help."

"I'll keep my thinking cap on."

"Don't ever take it off, Walter. So long now." Nelson hung up the phone and looked over at Vormbrock. "Let's take a ride over to Pearly Gates Cemetery. It's high time we paid our respects to Nicky's dead wife."

51

W ell, look who's back," the chatty waiter from the night before called out when Regan and Abigail walked into Jimbo's. "I
still haven't seen your friend."

"Don't worry about it," Regan said. "We're here to have a
quick glass of wine." She pointed. "It's Abigail's birthday."

"Well, Happy Birthday! You're a Capricorn."

"Yes, and I was born on Friday the thirteenth."

"Bummer! Do you two want to sit at one of my tables by the
window? I'll bring you a complimentary tray of birthday hors
d'oeuvres."

"Are you sure?" Abigail asked. "We don't want to take a table
when we're not ordering a meal."

"Yes! We won't get busy until after 5:00."

"Okay then."

"Would you like to sit at the table where your friend with the
gloves spent the night torturing me?"

"Why not?" Abigail laughed.

As he led them to the table, Abigail and Regan glanced at
each other. They were both thinking the same thing—this is
where Lois saw Cody.

"My name is Jonathan," the waiter told them as they sat down. "What can I get you to drink?"

They both ordered red wine.

"Two glasses of *vin rouge*, coming right up!" Jonathan sang out as he hurried off.

Abigail smiled, then turned to Regan. "I have to call Kaitlyn and Lois. But first I'd better figure out where we're going to eat tonight and make a reservation. I should have done that earlier."

Regan raised an eyebrow. "You've had a busy day."

"I'd say you have, too." Abigail scratched her head. "I'm trying to think of a restaurant that my grandmother and her friend will enjoy—nothing too noisy or expensive."

"There's a low-key Italian restaurant on Little Santa Monica Boulevard in Beverly Hills. I used to go there with my parents . . ."

"Ta-dah!"

They both turned. Jonathan was putting their glasses of wine down on the table. "I'll be right back."

Regan lifted her glass. "Happy Birthday, Abigail. I'm sorry about Cody. It's lousy you had to hear that news on your birthday."

"Regan, after what happened to you today, I could care less about Cody. I am just so grateful that you're okay." She paused. "But I do want my money back!"

They laughed and clicked glasses.

"Happy Birthday . . ." their waiter was singing playfully as he approached, then placed a tray of pigs in a blanket, cut-up vegetables, and tiny grilled-cheese sandwiches in front of them.

"Thank you," Abigail said. "You're so kind."

"I love making my customers feel good," he replied. "It

makes work so much more fun. Of course, when I get someone like your friend with the gloves . . ." He rolled his eyes.

Abigail smiled. "She couldn't have been that bad."

"Excuse me? That poor guy she was with. I think he escaped to the bathroom three times. I don't blame him one bit. You say he was a hand model, too?"

"That's what she said."

"Well, then let me tell you something. His hands must be the most attractive part of his body. I mean, please!"

"Regan," Abigail said, "remind me to never come here with Lois."

Jonathan waved his hand. "I'm just having fun. So, did you ever find your other friend? The hunky one?"

"No."

"Now there's a handsome devil."

"Don't remind me," Abigail said. "And 'devil' is the operative word."

"Love, ain't it grand?" Jonathan sighed. "What about you?" he asked Regan. "Is that a wedding band I see on your ring finger?"

"Yes, it is. I'm happy to say that I'm married to a great guy."

"That makes one of us."

"Believe me," Regan said. "He wasn't easy to find."

"The good ones never are," Jonathan replied.

"My ex isn't easy to find, and he's not good either," Abigail moaned.

"Oh dear," Jonathan said. "Your friend with the gloves seemed to like the guy she was with."

"Really?" Abigail asked. "She didn't mention anything about him except that they had dinner."

"I don't know. They seemed comfortable with each other,

which says something. Any normal human being would have been freaked out with all her complaining."

"They'd worked together all day," Abigail told him. "People get to know each other fast on those commercial shoots."

Two customers were walking through the door. "Excuse me," Jonathan said, turning away.

Regan and Abigail sipped their wine and ate their hors d'oeuvres, keeping an eye on the clock.

"We should get out of here soon," Regan finally said, signaling for the check. "Have you thought about whether we should make a reservation at that Italian restaurant?"

"Yes, but I decided we'd better wait to ask my grandmother what she wants to do. Believe me, if she's paying, she'll want to decide. She'll probably want a place that might provide her with a celebrity sighting."

"How about a place that might provide a Cody Castle sighting?"

"Wouldn't that be a nice birthday present?" Abigail asked. "But something tells me they don't have the same taste in restaurants."

52

Vormbrock and Nelson drove through the entrance of Pearly Gates Cemetery, passing rows and rows of tombstones on their way to the administration building.

"Look at all the different names," Nelson said. "Whenever I go to a burial, I keep an eye out to see if there are any Nelsons in the cemetery. I always spot one. It's a weird feeling."

"With a name like Vormbrock, I don't have that problem."

They parked near the office building, got out of the car, and paused for a moment. There was no one in sight. Flowers planted in front of headstones were blowing gently in the breeze.

"So this is where Nicky would visit his wife every Sunday," Nelson observed. "I wonder where her grave is."

"Let's go find out," Vormbrock said as they walked up the steps of the building.

Inside the door there was a small hallway that led to a large high-ceilinged room with four desks positioned closely together. Enormous windows overlooked the cemetery. Paperwork was piled everywhere. It appeared obvious that the two men and two women in the room worked as a group. That, or they didn't need much privacy.

A sweet-faced matronly woman greeted them. "Hello," she

said, getting up from her desk. She looked to be in her sixties and was obviously in charge. "My name is Beatrice. May I help you?" she asked, probably assuming they were interested in a plot.

Detective Nelson showed her his badge. "We wanted to ask a few questions about a man named Nicky Tendril. His wife is buried here . . ."

The three other employees looked up from their work.

"That poor man!" Beatrice exclaimed.

"Our sentiments exactly."

"We just heard the terrible news from his niece. Nicky will be buried right beside his wife, Abigail. He bought a plot for two when she died all those years ago. His death is such a shame. We're all in shock."

"You knew him then?"

"Everyone here knew Nicky," one of the men said, with a be-mused expression but not being unkind.

"We understand he came here every Sunday to visit his wife's grave," Nelson said.

Beatrice nodded solemnly. "Yes, he did. Because so many people visit their loved ones on Sunday, our office is open half a day. We like to be here if the relatives need us. Only one of us works and we take turns. We started this policy a few years ago and it's worked out beautifully. Especially for someone like Nicky."

"Especially for someone like Nicky," the other male employee repeated. "He always had something to complain about. Like if a blade of grass didn't look green enough."

"Aw," Beatrice said. "Nicky was a dear. And sometimes he had a right to complain. When he was here two days ago—"

"He was here two days ago?" Nelson asked.

"Sure. Two days ago was Sunday, wasn't it?"

Nelson nodded.

"Anyway, he came in to talk to me about the tree that stands behind his wife's tombstone. Sap from the tree was dripping onto the tombstone and getting it all messy. He wanted to get the tombstone cleaned immediately."

"Did he talk about anything else?"

"He said that maybe he should upgrade the headstone. Abigail's name was fading. Fifty years being exposed to the elements will do that." Beatrice shook her head. "He was sitting right here two days ago. Who'd have believed that the next time he came back would be for all of eternity?" she asked, staring up at Nelson.

"Yes, that is unbelievable," Nelson agreed. "Did Nicky ever have anybody with him when he came for his visits?"

"Never used to," Beatrice answered. "But the last two or three times I saw him he had a companion."

"Do you know who that was?

"I have no idea. She was a woman with red hair."

"Red hair?" Vormbrock asked calmly.

Beatrice lowered her voice, pretending to whisper. "I think it was a wig."

"Did you ever talk to her?"

"No. When Nicky came into the office he was always alone. I think his friend was trying to be respectful. The woman drove him to the cemetery and usually walked around while he visited his wife. She was obviously sensitive to his continuing heartache. This past Sunday when he was in here talking about the sap, she ducked in to use the ladies' room way over there." She pointed to the far wall.

"You weren't introduced?"

"No. We waved at each other when she walked in. She used the ladies' room and went right back outside. Of course I had to ask Nicky who she was. He joked that she was his Gal Friday.

I know it wasn't a girlfriend. How could it be? He was madly in love with his wife. It's so sad, I tell you. But at least they're together now."

"If you only saw her from a distance, how did you know she was wearing a wig?" Vormbrock asked.

"A little while after Nicky left the office, it was time to close up. When I drove out, I passed them. They'd gone back to his wife's gravesite. It was so windy. They were standing by the stone. Nicky was pointing at all the sap stains. I saw her wig start to blow off. She grabbed it just in time. I don't think Nicky even noticed."

"How was she dressed?"

"Respectfully, as one should when visiting the deceased. Black pants, a flowered blouse. She wore big sunglasses. Oh!" Beatrice said quickly, pointing her index finger in the air. "Wait . . . I have something she left behind in the bathroom."

"What would that be?" Nelson asked, his heart quickening.

Beatrice opened her drawer. "I put it in my desk and was planning to give it to whoever was going to work this Sunday and ask them to give it to Nicky." She pulled out a small white plastic bottle. "I can't tell whether it's a cream or a cleanser. What I can tell is that it must be expensive. It's not a prescription, but it comes from a doctor's office in Beverly Hills."

She handed the white plastic bottle to Nelson. "Don't you love that?" she asked with a giggle. "Dr. Cleary—Dermatologist to the Stars."

Nelson looked at Vormbrock, then back to Beatrice. "If you don't mind, I'll take this with us."

"Of course."

Nelson turned to the others who'd been hanging on every word. "Did any of you have contact with this red-haired woman?"

No one had spoken to her.

"What kind of car did she drive?"

Some kind of white sedan was all anyone remembered.

"Thank you for your time." Nelson turned to Beatrice and gave her his card. "If there's anything else you think of, or if Nicky's companion stops by here or calls, please let me know right away."

"Do you think that woman could have killed Nicky?" Beatrice asked, her eyes widening.

"I'm not saying that. We just want to talk to anyone who knew him," Nelson answered evasively. "By the way, where is Nicky's wife's grave?"

"Section 7. On the right-hand side of the road leading out to the gate."

Vormbrock and Nelson hurried back to the car. Vormbrock quickly started the engine. "You think we'll be having a chat with Gloria Carson sooner rather than later?" he asked as he backed out of the parking space.

"I hope so." Nelson held up the white plastic bottle. "I'm dying to know if this is cream or cleanser."

53

When Regan and Abigail got in the car outside of Jimbo's, Abigail called the airlines. "Oh my God, Regan, her flight is arriving early," Abigail lamented. "They must have picked up speed."

"How early?" Regan asked.

"Fifteen minutes. Maybe Grandma lent the captain her broom."

"Abigail!"

"I'm kidding. She's not a witch. I'm the witch, remember? My grandma is a nice woman. But she's tough and I'm scared."

"I thought all you could think about now is how happy you are that I'm still alive. Has that feeling of relief worn off already?" Regan asked with a smile.

Abigail laughed heartily. "I know in the grand scheme of things that this problem is not earth shattering. But wait till you meet her."

The traffic was predictably heavy. Every five minutes Abigail had Regan call to check the status of the flight.

"It's gained fifteen seconds," Regan said after the third call.

"I'm sorry, Regan. I know I'm being ridiculous. We'll get there when we get there."

The time was 4:38 when Abigail turned off the highway onto the road leading to the airport. "The flight lands in seven minutes," she said nervously.

"Drive straight to the baggage claim area," Regan instructed. "You get out and wait for her. I'll drive around. Call me when you've collected her bags."

"Okay."

Abigail pulled up to the curb, got out, and ran inside the terminal. She hurried to the area where friends, family, and drivers from car services waited for the passengers.

On a screen on the wall, the word ARRIVED was flashing next to her grandmother's flight number. It might as well say YOU'RE TOAST, Abigail thought as she caught her breath. Six minutes later the passengers started coming through. Lots of hugs and kisses.

Where is she? Abigail wondered. Then she spotted the woman whom she loved dearly but at the moment wished was thousands of miles away. Grandma Ethel was coming through the door with a guy who looked like a wrestler. He was carrying her purse and wheeling a flowered carry-on. She was clutching her big black umbrella that doubled as a walking stick.

"Grandma," Abigail called out, hurrying over.

"It's the birthday girl!" Ethel said, giving Abigail a hug. She turned to the man. "Shark, say hello to my granddaughter Abigail."

Shark looked less than thrilled. "Hello. Here," he said, handing over Ethel's belongings.

Abigail put the purse over her shoulder and grabbed the handle of the suitcase. "Thank you so very much," she said.

He grunted an inaudible response, and hurried off.

"We sat next to each other," Ethel said brightly. Her electric blue eyes were sparkling, each one accented with a slash of black eyeliner. That and one application of bright red lip-stick was enough fussing for Ethel. Her dark hair was slightly streaked with gray. She'd swear to anyone who'd listen that she had never ever colored her hair, even though she had a grand-daughter who'd do it for free. She had on her traveling outfit—sturdy shoes, black stretch pants, and an Indiana Hoosiers sweatshirt.

"Let's get your baggage, Grandma," Abigail said.

"What do you mean?"

"Didn't you check a bag?"

"No. I fit everything into that little suitcase. I've got a dress that doesn't wrinkle. I'll wear that tonight. How much stuff do I need?"

"Not a lot," Abigail agreed.

"Besides, I can't stay for that long. I came here to get a job done. I want to get you a nest, girl, and then I want to get back home."

Abigail felt sick to her stomach. "My friend is circling the airport. Let me call her."

"Who's your friend?"

"Regan Reilly. I used to live across the hall from her. She's visiting me for a few days."

Ethel frowned. "Didn't you tell me once she was a private investigator?"

"Did I mention that to you?"

"Sure did. I've got a mind like a steel trap. You should know that by now."

"Believe me, Grandma, I haven't forgotten."

Three minutes later Regan pulled up. Abigail introduced them. "I forgot that I'd told my grandmother about you last year. She remembers that you're a private investigator."

"Oh," Regan said. "Uh-huh."

"Must be interesting work," Ethel said, getting in the front seat as Regan got into the back. "Had any good cases lately?"

"A few," Regan answered.

"I'd love to hear all about them."

Abigail decided to immediately go in for the sympathy vote. "Grandma, Regan saved my life today."

Ethel gasped. "What?"

Abigail related the story.

"A stalker!" Ethel said incredulously.

"Yes."

Ethel frowned. "That's terrible. I hope you're okay, Regan."

"Yes, I am. Thank you."

"Makes me wonder if Mugs's apartment will be secure enough for you, Abigail."

"It might not be," Abigail replied a little too quickly.

Ethel reached into her purse, pulled out her notebook, and wrote "Security Issues—priceless" in it. "I've got a list here, honey, of everything I can think of that might save us a cent while we're negotiating the deal."

Abigail glanced in the rearview mirror at Regan, whose expression was priceless. I wish I had a camera, Abigail thought.

"I called Mugs when I landed," Ethel said, putting the notebook back in her purse. "I promised I would. Your father made me get a cell phone. I still have no idea how to use all the crazy doodads the kids think are so wonderful. Anyway, Mugs said to tell whoever you invited for dinner to come to her apartment first for a little birthday toast."

"That's very sweet," Abigail said. "I asked two girlfriends to join us tonight."

"Call them now. We'll start the celebration at what I hope will soon be your future home."

54

At 5:00, Gloria bolted from the office and drove home as fast as she could without speeding. Those two detectives would just love to see me pulled over, wouldn't they, she thought. It would prove to them that I'm a hopeless lawbreaker. I'm not only a murderer, but I also disobey traffic signs.

She turned down her block. The parking space she'd had yesterday, right in front of her apartment, was available. Score one, she thought. She parked quickly and got out.

Now I will do a reenactment of what happened yesterday, she told herself. Not a complete one, of course. I wouldn't go near Nicky's apartment with a ten-foot pole. Gloria threw her keys on the ground, leaned over and grabbed them, then straightened up. I know that something flickered in my brain when I did this yesterday, she thought. Did I see movement at Nicky's window? His bedroom window and one of his living room windows face this block. He had shades that he pulled down at night, but he also had sheer curtains that gave him a degree of privacy during the day. Did I see the curtain flutter? Am I grasping at straws?

Gloria sighed. Nicky was probably still alive when I got home.

I was home for half an hour before I went to do laundry. When I found him, they said he hadn't been dead for very long.

If only I'd decided to do the wash sooner.

Gloria turned, walked across the sidewalk, then slowly ascended the four steps to her apartment. She retrieved her mail from the mailbox on the wall next to her front door, then unlocked the door and went inside.

She placed the mail on the hallway table, went into the kitchen to pour herself a cold drink, then turned on the television to check the news. None of her activities were ringing any bells.

The key to the laundry shed was hanging on a hook by her back door. She scooped up a load of towels, took the key in her hand, and walked outside. The drab feeling of the tiny, paved backyard was softened by the numerous potted plants the tenants all contributed. A rickety glass table with three chairs completed the decor.

Gloria unlocked the door of the shed and stepped inside. She took three steps to the washing machine, lifted the lid, and laughed out loud. The machine was filled with clothes. I don't know why we bother with that sign, she thought, looking up. People remove their clothes immediately only if they sit here and read, and nobody seems to do that. She looked down at the basket of magazines and newspapers on the floor to the right of the machine. They were left there by tenants who no longer had use for them. Many of the magazines were so old that they really belonged in a recycling bin, Gloria often thought.

But the gossip paper on top was surprisingly recent. One of the headlines was about yet another celebrity who had overdone the Botox. Gloria reached down and picked it up.

When she saw the reading material that was now at the top of the pile, she gasped.

"This is it!" she cried, leaning down and picking up a script. The words NOTHING BUT GARBAGE were scrawled above the title in Nicky's handwriting. Gloria recognized the handwriting of everyone in the building. Collecting monthly rent checks made her a handwriting expert.

The script was called UNTITLED.

Gloria opened to the first page. Inside was a handwritten note on a plain sheet of white paper.

Dear Mr. Tendril,
We hope you enjoy our script and are so looking forward to coming to your home to discuss your involvement in our production.

Sincerely,
Dean Puntler

Gloria looked at the cover page of the script. Whoever Dean Puntler is, wrote this, she realized. He and someone named Cody Castle. Had they been here yesterday? Gloria left the shed, quickly locked the door, and ran back inside her apartment. I've got to call those detectives, she thought wildly, looking around for the card they had given her.

Her doorbell rang. She raced to answer it. Detective Nelson and Detective Vormbrock were standing on her porch.

"Oh!" she cried. "I'm so glad you're here. I have something to show you."

"That's funny," Nelson said. "We have something to show you, too." That tone of voice again! Gloria thought angrily. It was so aggravating. She'd show them. "Come in, please," she said as civilly as she could.

They took the same seats in her living room they had the previous day.

Gloria ran to the kitchen and got the script. She ran back

and held it up for them. "I just found this in the laundry room. I knew I saw something that struck me as unusual yesterday."

She handed the script to Nelson. Did she detect a surprised reaction?

"Look at that note!" she said. "Maybe that Dean was here yesterday!"

Nelson and Vormbrock's faces remained impassive.

"Will you try and get in touch with him'?" Gloria asked excitedly. "Or that other guy? That Cody Castle? I know there's no phone number but there must be a way of finding them."

"We'll look into that."

Frustration was building inside Gloria. They didn't seem to care that she might have found the murderers.

Detective Nelson pulled a clear plastic bag out of his pocket. The bag contained a white plastic bottle. "Does this look familiar?" he asked, holding it up.

Gloria frowned. "Yes. It's from Dr. Cleary's line of skin care products."

"Do you use this product?"

"It depends on which one it is."

Keeping the bag in his hand, Nelson brought it closer to Gloria's face. She looked at the numbers on the label. "That's an extra-strength lotion," she said. "I would never use that. Very few people do."

"Are you sure?"

"Of course I'm sure. Go look in my cabinet. I use two of Dr. Cleary's creams that are made for delicate skin."

"You use fancy creams, wear nice makeup, dress well," Nelson said. "Do you ever bother with a wig? Maybe on those days your hair doesn't look right?"

"What are you talking about?"

"Someone accompanied Nicky Tendril out to his wife's grave

on Sunday. She left this lotion behind in the bathroom of the office. Apparently she was wearing a red wig."

Adrenaline shot through Gloria's body. "That wasn't me!" she cried. "And I have proof! There was a dermatologists' convention in Long Beach on Sunday. Everyone from Dr. Cleary's office was at the booth all day peddling his products! I was there from 8:00 in the morning until 8:00 at night!" she screamed, then ran to the phone. "I'll call him for you right now! Right now!"

Nelson and Vormbrock jumped to their feet. "Please calm down," Nelson said. "Please."

Reluctantly Gloria put down the phone.

"Maybe you can help us," Vormbrock said.

"That's what I've been trying to do."

"Can you get the names of everyone who bought this lotion from Dr. Cleary?"

"Of course. It could take some time but it's probably on the computer at the office."

Nelson smiled. "*Now* I'd appreciate it if you called your boss. Ask him if he would open up his office for us."

"You're in luck. He works until 8:00 tonight."

"That's great. Could you come with us right away?"

"What about those guys who wrote the script? Don't you have any interest in finding them?"

"More than you know. We're going to call the station and report what you found. Are you ready to go?"

"I'll get my purse," Gloria sniffed.

55

I love a hen party," Mugs said gleefully as she passed around a tray of melon balls with prosciutto. "To have you girls here in my home reminds me of the old days when Harry and I used to entertain."

"Your apartment is lovely," Regan said, then was sure Grandma Ethel shot her a dirty look.

Mugs beamed. "You think so?"

"Oh yes," Regan gulped.

"I love being right by the pool, having a terrace, the feeling of a resort," Mugs continued, sounding like a real estate agent.

"The kitchen floor needs to be replaced," Ethel noted as she helped herself to a bowl of peanuts.

Hopefully they'll spend days haggling about the price, Regan thought. It buys us time to find Cody.

Kaitlyn and Lois had arrived at the same time. They were both friendly, but Kaitlyn seemed subdued. She said she'd fought terrible traffic on her way up from Orange County and had had a tough day at work. Lois wasn't nearly as bad as Regan expected, but true to form she had on a pair of long gloves. Tonight they were black, with glittery threads running through the material.

The group had already discussed the stalker in great detail. It was nearly 7:30 and they had an 8:00 reservation at a family-style restaurant on La Cienega Boulevard.

I can't imagine how Abigail is feeling, Regan thought, glancing over at her. She was seated next to her grandmother on the couch. This is a lovely apartment that would be perfect for her. Now that she's seen how charming it is, the whole situation must be eating her up inside. She must be frantic to get back out and look for Cody.

Regan's cell phone rang. She glanced down. It was a Los Angeles number. "Excuse me," she said, as she got up and walked out on the terrace.

It was Detective Nelson.

"Ms. Reilly, I've got good news."

Regan's pulse quickened. "What?" she asked quickly.

"We've located Cody Castle."

The words sent an electrical charge through Regan's body. "Where is he?"

"It's a long story. Last night his writing partner lost a bag containing their script and a lot of paperwork. It was found by a cop outside the police station a little while ago. They went through the bag at the station and found the partner's date book. My colleagues knew that Detective Vormbrock and I were interested in talking to these guys and got in touch with me immediately. I called Dean and said we had the bag, and told him that I glanced at the script and thought it was so interesting . . ."

Regan smiled. "He fell for the bait?"

"Hook, line, and sinker. But, Ms. Reilly, there's something else. You and I are interested in finding Castle for different reasons. Mine just got more serious. A copy of their script was found in the laundry room at Nicky Tendril's apartment."

Regan's eyes widened. "It was?"

"Yes. As we know, that doesn't necessarily mean anything but . . ."

"Where is Castle?" Regan asked.

"I was getting to that. He and his partner will be having a business dinner with one of their investors at the Polo Lounge tonight."

"The Polo Lounge! That's less than a ten-minute drive from where we are now."

"They have a 7:30 reservation. Dean told me they were hoping to make it a quick dinner. I volunteered to bring the bag to him. He asked if I could join them for a drink. He was so thrilled that I loved the script, and even asked if I could mention how much I enjoyed it to the investor."

"Unbelievable," Regan said, "So you'll be there."

"Yes. Right now my partner and I are following up another lead, then we'll head over. We'll be there by 8:00."

"You wouldn't mind if we decided to have Abigail's birthday dinner at 8:00 at the Polo Lounge, now would you?"

"Not at all. I'd be delighted."

"See you there."

"Regan, what's going on?" Abigail asked, stepping out onto the terrace.

Regan faced her. "You have to promise not to faint."

"I promise."

"That was Detective Nelson. A copy of Cody and Dean's script was found in the laundry room at Nicky's apartment building."

Abigail grabbed the railing. "What?"

"You heard me. But wait, it gets better—Cody and Dean will be having a business dinner tonight at the Polo Lounge with an investor."

Abigail took her hand off the railing and grabbed Regan's

arm. "How do we do this?" she asked excitedly. "I don't want to tell my grandmother in front of her friend that I don't have the money anymore. But, gee, if we go to the Polo Lounge I just might get it back." Abigail paused. "Regan, we can't just leave Grandma and Mugs here on my birthday. We have that other reservation. And I think the Polo Lounge might be a little expensive for my grandmother . . ."

"I've got an idea," Regan said.

"What?"

"You say I saved your life today?"

"Yes."

"That means I'm responsible for you."

"It does?"

"Yes. It's some old proverb. Anyway, I'll go inside and announce that tonight I want to take everyone to dinner. Since I saved your life, I'm responsible for you, and I really want to host your celebration tonight, and I think the perfect place would be the Polo Lounge. Do you think your grandmother would go for it?"

"If it means she wouldn't have to pay, of course she would."

Regan laughed.

"You can tell them whatever you want, Regan, but obviously I will pay you back."

"Don't worry about that now. If we find Cody, it will all be worth it. But we have to be careful."

"Regan," Abigail said softly. "I can't believe that after three months I'm actually going to see him."

"You're not softening, are you?" Regan asked.

"No. I still want to tear him limb from limb. I won't be able to do that, but I can't wait to show his investor the IOU."

"Good. You have the IOU handy?"

"Of course. It's in my purse."

Regan squeezed Abigail's good hand. "We're in this together, kid."

They went back inside and Regan made her announcement.

"The Polo Lounge!" Mugs cried. "Harry and I used to love to go there for a drink."

"But I was going to treat everyone tonight," Ethel said half-heartedly.

"Like your granddaughter, I'm a little superstitious," Regan said. "I really think I need to buy her dinner tonight."

"Fine."

Lois adjusted her gloves. "I love the Polo Lounge. It's so elegant and truly reminds me of old-world Hollywood."

"The Polo Lounge sounds great to me," Kaitlyn said with a smile. She lifted her glass. "It's just so wonderful for all of us to be together for your birthday, Abigail."

"Hopefully you'll be together again on Abigail's birthday next year," Mugs said, nodding her head. "Sitting right here in Abigail's home."

"We'll see," Ethel answered. "I noticed the bathroom faucet has a little leak . . ."

56

Cody had ordered *Gone with the Wind* from pay-per-view and only started watching it with Stella at 6:30. He knew it was her favorite movie, but what really interested him was that it was four hours long.

"When are we going to go out?" Stella asked before the movie began.

"As soon as it's over," he said breezily.

Stella giggled. "That won't be until 10:30."

"No problem. The clubs don't get going until then."

At 7:25, Cody got up from the couch.

"What are you doing?" Stella asked.

"I'll be right back."

"Where are you going?"

"I have a little surprise planned for you."

"You do?"

He laughed. "Yes, I do."

"I love surprises. You promise you'll be right back?"

"I promise. Now shhhh. Watch the movie," he said as he disappeared out the door.

57

G reat work," Detective Nelson said to Gloria. They were in a back room at Dr. Cleary's office. Computer records showed that only five patients had purchased the extra-strength cream in the past year. "We'll start checking out these ladies right away." He looked at Vormbrock. "Ready to go?"

"What about me?" Gloria asked. "Are you forgetting I rode over here with you?"

"No," Nelson said. "I'm not. Sorry. I've got a lot on my mind." He looked at his watch. "We're running tight on time. We have to pick something up at the station, and drop it off at the Polo Lounge, and then—"

"You can drop me off at the Polo Lounge, too," Gloria interrupted. "If anyone could use a stiff drink, it's yours truly."

58

Abigail's heart was beating wildly as she drove her grandmother, Regan, and Mugs over to the Polo Lounge. Kaitlyn and Lois were following in their own cars. Thank God Regan had been able to get a last-minute reservation.

This is surreal, Abigail thought. Grandma Ethel is in the backseat, blissfully unaware that she is about to be in the same room with a man who absconded with her money. I never thought the search for Cody would come to this.

It was 7:55.

"Here we are," Abigail croaked as she turned off Sunset Boulevard and pulled up the driveway of the Beverly Hills Hotel.

Mugs inhaled. "Ohhh," she breathed. "It's all so beautiful. Ethel, look at the palm trees."

"I see them."

"We'll have to come back during the day. The flowers are just exquisite. And the gardens in the back are lush and beautiful." Mugs laughed. "This hotel is what they call The Pink Palace. It's the place to see and be seen."

Never more true than tonight, Regan thought. She turned and winked at Abigail.

"I read somewhere that Elizabeth Taylor honeymooned with

six of her eight husbands in the bungalows out back," Mugs informed them.

"My word," Ethel replied. "It's very nice of you to bring us here, Regan."

"An absolute treat!" Mugs agreed. "I'm so excited."

"My pleasure," Regan said, feeling slightly guilty. If they only knew.

Abigail stopped the car at the entrance. Valets quickly opened all the doors and welcomed them to the hotel.

Lois and Kaitlyn pulled up behind them.

The six women walked into the hotel lobby together.

"Isn't this lovely, Ethel?" Mugs asked, pointing to the elegant, colorful décor. "I adore the pinks and the greens . . . It feels so tropical . . . and so peaceful."

59

As much as Stella loved *Gone with the Wind*, tonight she was losing interest. The first hour was wonderful, while Cody was cuddled beside her. But now she was furious. He'd been gone for half an hour. Where did he go?

She tried his cell phone but he didn't pick up.

What is going on? she wondered. What surprise could take so long? This is getting ridiculous. First he keeps me waiting last night at the airport, then he doesn't care that I was scared to death after the earthquake, today he's gone for most of the day, and now he's disappeared.

She punched the cushion on the couch and frowned.

What would Scarlett O'Hara do?

60

Right this way, ladies," the maître d' instructed.

Across the plush, softly lit room, Abigail spotted Cody, Dean, and an older couple sitting in a booth, deep in conversation.

"There he is," Lois whispered to Abigail and Regan.

"I know," Abigail said tersely. "Let's get my grandmother seated before we do anything."

"Is this satisfactory?" the maître d' asked, stopping at a semi-circular booth directly across the room from Cody's.

"It's perfect," Abigail answered.

"Regan, do you mind if Mugs and I slide in first?" Ethel asked. "I think we'd both love a view of the action."

"Of course not," Regan answered. I only hope it's not too much action, she thought.

The waiter came and took their drink orders.

"Grandma, Mugs, would you excuse us for a minute?" Abigail asked. "Regan and I want to talk to someone at the table over there." She pointed across the room.

"I want to say hello, too," Lois said, her tone slightly annoyed.

"Come on then."

Kaitlyn tried to pretend that nothing was happening. "So, Mrs. Feeney, are you enjoying yourself so far?"

"It's wonderful. Mugs and I are so glad to see each other, right, Mugs?"

"Right!"

As Abigail was approaching Cody's table, flanked by her two friends, the woman at the table looked up and smiled expectantly. The three men turned their heads toward her at the same time. Predictably, Cody and Dean looked as if they'd just come unglued.

"Hello there," Abigail began. "How to nice to see you, Cody. Dean . . . and . . . ?"

Introductions were made all around.

Thomas Pristavec was smiling broadly. "You know these two guys? I'm so excited about their movie."

"Really?" Abigail answered.

"Yes. I think the script is wonderful." Pristavec laughed. "They talked me into investing. I couldn't be more excited."

Abigail pulled the IOU out of her pocket. "I have something you might be interested in seeing before you give them any of your money."

"Abigail!" Cody growled.

"Cody owes me one hundred thousand dollars. I lent it to him last October and then he disappeared. The loan is due today." She smiled. "My birthday."

Thomas looked at the IOU and then at Cody. "Is this true?" he asked, appalled.

Cody's mouth twitched. "I was planning to pay it back. I . . . I . . ."

"How about right now?" Abigail asked, opening her hand and extending her palm.

"Cody—there you are! I've been looking all over for you," a woman cried accusingly.

They all turned as a young, beautiful blonde charged toward the group. "Cody, what is going on here?" she demanded in a voice that would carry to the back of any theater.

The maître d' hurried over to shush her.

"Don't shush me!"

Oh my God, Regan thought, she's the actress I saw at the airport last night.

"Cody, what's going on here? You disappeared on me!" she spat.

"He has a habit of doing that," Abigail announced. "Just be sure you don't lend him any money."

"Lend him money?" Stella squeaked.

"I was his girlfriend until he disappeared in October, right after I lent him one hundred thousand dollars."

"He's horrible!" Lois added enthusiastically. "A real creep. If I were you, I'd run for your life."

"I can explain everything, Stella!" Cody insisted. "Please."

Pristavec pounded the table. "I thought you told us Stella was in New York."

"Who are you?" Stella demanded.

"I was planning to invest in their film. I was about to hand over a check for fifty thousand dollars, but thanks to this lady here," he said, pointing to Abigail, "I realize there are better ways to spend my money!"

Slight moans were escaping from Dean's lips.

"I want my money, Cody!" Abigail said angrily. She pointed across the room. "Grandma Ethel is sitting right over there. You know she gave me that money to buy a home! She worked hard for every penny!"

"I worked hard for my money, too," Pristavec cried out. "And to think I almost handed it over to these two nitwits."

"Hey!" Dean shouted. "Don't put me in the same category as this guy!"

"Then what are you doing working with him?" Thomas asked. "If you have a partner who you know is a cheat, then you're a cheat, too."

"We'd already written the script when he was—"

"When he was what?" Stella and Abigail asked at once.

"When he was thrown in jail," a male voice answered from behind them.

They turned. It was Detective Nelson, followed by Detective Vormbrock. Nelson was carrying a black nylon bag.

"Thrown in jail for what?" Stella screeched.

"Moving violations. Lots of traffic tickets. Expired license. A missed court date. He spent sixty days in the slammer in Texas. He got sprung just in time for Christmas."

So that explains it, Regan thought.

"Let me introduce myself. I'm Detective Nelson from the LAPD and this is my partner, Detective Vormbrock. Which one of you is Dean?"

"Over here," Dean said meekly, raising his hand.

"Here's the bag you lost with all your important papers. I'm glad one of our officers found it on the street."

Dean slowly shook his head in disbelief. "It was stolen out of my car."

"Whatever. I'd love to have a chat with you and Cody when you finish dessert." Nelson tapped Cody's arm. "You must be Cody, huh?"

Cody barely nodded.

"Why do you want to talk to them?" Thomas demanded.

Nelson shrugged. "A man whom they solicited to invest in their film was murdered."

"Murdered?" Kicky shrieked.

"Murdered?" Stella sobbed.

"Murdered!" Abigail repeated vehemently.

"Murdered!" Lois spat.

"I did not murder that man!" Cody shouted. His face was turning beet red. "I might owe Abigail money, and I might act like a jerk sometimes, but I am not a murderer!"

Gloria had seated herself at the bar not far from Dean and Cody's booth. I'm glad I didn't miss this, she thought. She slid off the stool and moved closer to the action. Like everyone in the room she was focused on the showdown. She couldn't believe the actress who had come to the office today was in the middle of this uproar. Dr. Cleary certainly gets some interesting patients.

"That night we met you, I knew you were capable of anything!" Lois seethed, glaring at Cody. "I told Abigail she should never have given you the time of day!"

Gloria turned her head and stared at the woman who had just vented her negative feelings. That voice and that negativity was so familiar. It was the woman with the gloves speaking.

"Oh, be quiet!" Dean shouted at Lois. "You were insufferable from the moment we met you. Look at you, still wearing gloves." He turned to Kicky. "You're normal. This woman is insane."

"How dare you?" Thomas cried. "Why are you bringing Kicky into this display of human treachery?"

Dean waved his hand. "They're both hand models."

Kicky turned her head and looked at Lois. "You're a hand model?"

"Yes, I am," Lois answered.

"Who's your agent?"

"Kicky, I don't think this is the time for that," Thomas reprimanded.

"I'm sorry, Thomas."

Dean glared at Lois. "You haven't answered the question."

"It's none of your business," Lois snapped.

"Kicky was asking, not me. Why don't you tell her who your agent is?"

I can't believe it, Gloria thought. I know who that woman with the gloves is! I'd recognize that complaining voice anywhere. Her hair color is different, but I know it's her. Gloria tugged on Nelson's arm and whispered in his ear.

Nelson stared straight ahead as he listened.

"If you have such beautiful hands then why don't you show them to us?" Dean demanded. "I bet your hands aren't as beautiful as Kicky's!"

"You make me sick," Lois said with disgust.

"Come on," Nelson encouraged Lois. "Take off the gloves and show him how beautiful your hands are. If you have gorgeous hands, you should show them off. No sense waiting until you're ready for the Pearly Gates . . ."

As Lois's head swiveled in Nelson's direction, her eyes met the stare of the woman standing next to him. She turned and ran.

But she didn't get very far.

61

What in tarnation?" Ethel cried. "Mugs, slide over. I want to see what's going on!"

In her effort to escape, Lois shoved a waiter who was carrying a tray of tropical drinks. Peach slices, berries, and glasses of sugary sweet liquid went flying. She stumbled and started to fall. Nelson grabbed her arm.

"What's your hurry?" he asked.

Lois scowled at him.

"We're going to have to arrest you for disorderly conduct. The thing is, you'll have to take those gloves off before we slap on the handcuffs."

Dean climbed over Cody to get out of the booth. "I've got to see this."

"Regan, I can't take it," Abigail whispered.

Lois started to cry as she yanked off the gloves. Her hands were rough and irritated, the nails worn down to the quick. A jagged purple scar ran across the top of her right hand.

No wonder she needed that lotion, Ethel thought. Look what happens when you don't use it for two days. The redness comes right back.

"Who's your agent?" Dean sneered. "Which hand is Meryl and which is Angelina?"

"Shut up!" Lois yelled. "I hope your movie never gets made!" She looked over at Abigail. "I'm sorry. I started wearing gloves after my hand was slashed a couple of years ago. Someone asked me if I was a hand model. I got carried away. At first it was fun . . ."

Abigail just stared at her in disbelief. "What do you do for a living?"

"I clean houses . . ."

"You clean for anyone under eighty years old?" Nelson asked sarcastically. "I doubt it. I can't wait to hear what you do with your free time, besides, of course, accompanying elderly people like Nicky Tendril to their spouse's gravesite every weekend. Let's go." He turned to Dean. "By the way, if you write a script on your own, I'd be happy to take a look at it."

Dean gave him the thumbs up.

The whole room was still as Lois was handcuffed and led away by Vormbrock and Nelson.

Cody broke the silence. "Abigail, I'm sorry. I promise I'll pay you back tomorrow. I'll borrow the money from my mother. All of a sudden, she's trying to make up for my miserable child-hood."

"I'm leaving!" Stella cried. She turned on her heels and flounced out dramatically.

Ethel hurried over to Abigail's side and put her arm protec-tively around her granddaughter. "What have we here?" she asked.

"Grandma, this is Cody. I lent him the money you gave me to buy a house. Then he disappeared. I didn't want to tell you . . ."

Ethel smacked Cody on the side of the head. "That's no way to treat my granddaughter."

"I know that. I'm sorry. I promise I'll pay her back tomorrow."

"You're a disgrace."

"Grandma, I'm sorry. I never should have . . ."

Ethel kissed Abigail's cheek. "No you shouldn't have, honey, but we all make mistakes. You've been through enough today. Let's go back to the booth and order dinner. I'm hungry! I never eat this late."

Abigail turned to Regan. "Ready for dinner?"

"I sure am," Regan said with a smile. "Now we can really celebrate your birthday."

Ethel and Abigail turned and started walking arm in arm back to the booth. "Honey, I remember the day you were born," Ethel was saying. "Even though it was Friday the thirteenth, we were all so thrilled . . ."

Regan turned to Cody, who couldn't look her in the eye. "I know you say you'll pay Abigail. But I'm a little less trusting than she is. Can I have your contact information, please?"

Dean whipped out his business card. "Here's my number and address. I'll make it my personal business to insure that Cody pays Abigail back every cent!"

Regan took both their cards and turned away. Her eyes met the openmouthed stare of the woman who had identified Lois. "Would you like to join us for dinner?" Regan asked. "We have an extra place at the table."

"I'd love to!" Gloria said quickly.

"Head on over to the booth. I think I'd better call my husband."

Wednesday, January 14th

62

By the next morning, numerous sorry details about Lois had come to light. Abigail and Regan were in Brennan's kitchen sipping coffee when Detective Nelson called to fill them in.

"Do you mind if I put you on speaker phone?" Abigail asked.

"Not at all. Make yourselves comfortable. That woman had a lot to say. She must be hoping for leniency."

Abigail and Regan sat across from each other, listening to an account of the dastardly deeds of someone who Abigail had considered a friend.

Lois used several aliases and disguises. Wigs and various kinds of clothing and makeup were found in the trunk of her car. She played many different roles in her attempts to get close to elderly people. Cleaning houses, offering rides, assistance in paying bills. She gained their trust, drained their bank accounts, and then was on her way.

When Lois learned that Nicky Tendril was a millionaire, she tracked his movements for a couple of weeks, following him to the Pearly Gates Cemetery two Sundays in a row. On the following Sunday, she waited for Nicky at the cemetery and introduced herself when he was at his wife's grave. She told him that her mother was buried in Pennsylvania, and she couldn't visit her grave very often. Because she felt so bad, she came to the Pearly Gates on Sundays to walk among the tombstones, praying for all the departed, particularly her mother.

Lois was jealous of Abigail. Even though Abigail said she was cursed, it seemed to Lois she had a much easier life. Abigail always got the attention from guys when they went out. She liked her job. Had fun on the set. Had friends. She didn't have to hide who she was. It frustrated Lois, who felt like she never got a break, so she purposely did things to trip Abigail up. Like having someone call and tell Abigail that mattresses were to be delivered to a home she was house-sitting at a time when Abigail was desperate to find Cody. But the most surprising thing of all was the identity of the man who made that call.

"Who was that?" Abigail interrupted.

"A guy named Oscar. Your friend Kaitlyn's boss."

Abigail's jaw dropped. She shook her head and continued listening.

Oscar's number was on the speed dial of Lois's cell phone and records showed that she called him and he called her several times a day. Lois had met him when she tagged along with Abigail on a trip to the Orange Grove facility. She didn't want to miss any opportunity to visit a place where there would be vulnerable elderly people. When she and Oscar were introduced, there was an immediate connection. The police were now checking into Oscar's background and the possibility of fraudulent Medicare claims emanating from his office at Orange Grove.

Oscar had been with Lois at Jimbo's the night Lois saw Cody. He told her she shouldn't bother to tell Abigail she'd seen Cody.

Most important, Lois confessed to Nicky Tendril's murder, though she claimed it was an accident. She had parked the car near Nicky's apartment and was shocked when she saw Dean running out the door. Then Cody. Once they were gone, Lois went inside. Nicky was anxious and upset, but so was she. They were in the kitchen. She asked Nicky why the two men had been there. He waved his hand at her and told her it was none of her business. She had come to pick up five thousand dollars that she was supposedly going to use to have a special new headstone made for his wife. She picked the envelope of cash off the counter and started to stuff it into her purse. Nicky blew up. "Everyone wants to take my money!" he yelled as he grabbed her bag.

Lois gave him a shove. She swears she never intended to kill him.

Regan and Abigail looked at each other.

"Poor Nicky," Abigail said.

"One more thing, Abigail," Nelson continued, "Nicky wasn't the one who wrote 'witch' on your picture."

Abigail was silent for a moment. "I'm really happy to hear that," she said softly.

63

For the second night in a row, Regan, Abigail, and Kaitlyn gathered at Mugs's apartment. They were there to celebrate the successful conclusion of intense negotiations between Mugs and Ethel over the purchase price of the apartment and also to toast the fact that Cody had actually handed over the money. His mother had wired him the funds. She was vacationing in Palm Beach, Florida, but had managed to get it done immediately. Abigail and Regan had met Cody in a supermarket parking lot where he was holding a certified check. Abigail couldn't help but ask about the movie. Pristavec hadn't pulled out, because he felt sorry for Dean and had already planned his screening party. But Dean and Cody had to hurry and find a new star. Stella was already back in New York.

Gloria was also in attendance, proud of herself for recognizing Lois.

Walter had been invited to join the ladies tonight and was in his glory. "I just knew if I called a meeting, we'd figure out something that would help the police. I just wish I'd been there at the Polo Lounge to see it all unfold . . ."

"It was something," Mugs said. "When the two detectives

walked in, I couldn't believe it. And then Abigail knew them! It was crazy."

"I still can't understand why you didn't tell us yesterday that your friend had been murdered," Ethel said.

"But, Ethel," Mugs answered, "I hadn't seen you in so long, and it was Abigail's birthday. It's a sad story. I didn't want that to be the first thing I brought up . . ."

Kaitlyn was in shock about her boss. "Last night I said it was a tough day at work. You should have seen it today. Federal agents were swarming the place."

Regan looked over at Abigail. With all she's been through, she finally looks at peace, Regan thought. This apartment will be perfect for her.

And Walter and Ethel seemed to be hitting it off. They were sitting next to each other on the couch, smiling and laughing. They truly looked as if they'd both been shot by Cupid's bow. Abigail caught Regan's gaze, subtly pointed to the two of them, and grinned.

Regan's cell phone rang. "It's Jack." She walked out to the terrace and flipped open her phone.

"Hey there."

"Hey yourself. You didn't come across any stalkers today, did you?"

"Not a one."

"Any more earthquakes?"

"Nope."

"I miss you."

"I miss you, too."

"You didn't decide to move back to Los Angeles, did you?"

"Not a chance."

Abigail appeared at the terrace door. "Tell Jack that thanks to you, I no longer feel cursed!"

Regan laughed. "I will. Jack, did you hear that?"

"I did. So now that Abigail's curse has been lifted, are you ready to come home?"

"I certainly am."

"What do you think of flying to Miami tomorrow? We'll stay for the weekend and get some sun. The weather in New York is lousy."

"I'd love that," Regan said.

"Good. I already bought your ticket."

"Perfect!"

"You sure? If you don't get the rest of your stuff out of your mother's garage before she gets back, you might end up cursed."

Regan laughed. "No I won't, Jack. Not if I'm with you . . ."

Three months later

64

Regan and Jack were in their bedroom getting ready to go to a NYC Police Foundation Gala at the Waldorf Hotel. Luke and Nora were meeting them there. Regan's cell phone rang as she was combing her hair.

She walked over to the dresser and picked up her phone. "Oh, it's Abigail. I haven't talked to her in a while."

"Regan, please," Jack said as he adjusted his tie. "I'm begging you. Don't answer it. It's been so peaceful . . ."

With a laugh, Regan waved her hand at him dismissively. "Hello."

"Regan!"

"Hi, Abigail. How are you?"

"I'm starting work on a movie next week, thank God. I'm using the money from my settlement to redo my kitchen. But I have to tell you, the curse is back!"

"The curse is back?" Regan repeated, surprise in her voice.

Jack's head whipped around from the mirror. He stared at Regan, shaking his head. "Hang up," he mouthed.

"Yes! I'm cursed again. Walter and my grandmother just got engaged. She's moving to Los Angeles. His apartment is two blocks away!"

Regan exhaled, as she burst out laughing. "Is that all?"

"Yup." Abigail chuckled.

"That's really good news. I'm so happy for them."

"Me, too. I don't have to worry about her bothering me. She won't have time! They're planning a cruise for their honeymoon, then a trip to Florida to visit Mugs, then they want to hit Niagara Falls before the year is out. The two of them are like teenagers. I'm going to have an engagement party for them next month. Any chance you and Jack can make it?"

"Gee, Abigail," Regan began, "I'm just not sure. We'll try . . ."

"It would be great if you were here." Abigail paused. "I've been dating this fanastic guy who I want you and Jack to meet. He's wonderful, I know he is. But if you two give him your seal of approval, I'll feel much better."

"Abigail, I know you've been burned, but if you really think he's that wonderful, you should trust your instincts."

"I know, Regan. But there is one problem."

Regan braced herself. "What?"

"He has thirteen letters in his name!"